Sky Joust:

The Purple Onion vs.
The Pestilence

Sky Joust:
The Purple Onion vs.
The Pestilence

A Novel

WILL MADDEN

SQUARE STRAW PRESS
Nashville, TN

Printed in the United States of America

First Printing, 2018

ISBN 978-0-9981404-9-0
Square Straw Press
Nashville, TN

Who reminded me of the crimes of my infancy?
For in his sight, none is innocent, not even
the infant who has lived but a day upon this earth.
Who reminded me? What were my crimes,
for which I hung upon the breast and wept?
Yay, I say onto you, it's the Onion who reminded me,
and I wept like goddamn fool.

—Augustine of Hippo

CONTENTS

EPISODE ONE:

PRELUDE TO A WAILING

MOONLIGHT shone through the ruined dome of the abandoned church. Its broad arc, vaulted high above the chancel, once bore a glittering mosaic of obsidian glass. Today, it lay below in shattered pieces, destroyed in the nineteenth century by the wrath of cannons.

Around the circular altar, three riders sat reverently upon their mounts. They held torches, the flickering tongues of flame offering a halo of warmth in the frosty mountain air. In leather pants and boots, the men had stripped to the waist. Their faces and chests were covered in war paint. Across the expanse of their shoulders and backs, each displayed a richly colored heraldic tattoo: a wildebeest, a heron, a judge.

The horses wore their best barding, the traditional hock-length ceremonial silks of equestrian church dress. No services had been held here in generations.

The torchlight crackled. Vapor billowed from the nostrils of man and animal alike.

"Why can't we just meet at the pub?" said the rider with the wildebeest tattoo. The stockiest of the three, he sat upon a horse in red barding. From the half-moon of his balding scalp, a dark tangle of hair fell to his shoulders.

Upon a blue-barded horse, a second rider stirred—the judge. "Favor your tongue, Sir Abhoc," he said. As in, give it a rest. *Shut up.* This was the tall one, whose well-muscled body bore signs of the most disciplined training.

"But we're missing the damn game, Sir Heckley!" Abhoc retorted. "The Pharaohs play the Knockjocks at home tonight. Mark Savory is pitching."

Heckley had TiVoed it but didn't want to invite Abhoc over to watch it with him. "Lord Brum wants to show us something," he said instead.

"I don't know why he can't show us in town," said the other.

"Horses are banned in town, Sir Abhoc," Heckley replied quietly. His mount snorted beneath him. *Idiot*, as if to say.

"Or why there can't be hot wings! Has anyone told Lord Brum what a pain in the ass it is to dress a horse?"

"We're Horsefolk," said Heckley with dignity.

"Well, is *he*? Doesn't he know I can't just throw all this barding in the washing machine when I get home?"

2

"You just need a bigger appliance," said Heckley.

The torchlight wavered. Leather creaked in the saddle.

"That's not what your wife told me last night," said Abhoc, leering.

"Aw now," Heckley shot back, "she always did do too much charity work." He smiled over at their third, a smaller freckle-faced man whose saddle seemed to swallow him. "Isn't that right, Sir Bubo?"

Bubo startled, surprised to hear his name. His horse wore green; he, the heron. "Yes, of course, Sir Heckley. Although if it helps, Sir Abhoc, I can procure an industrial-sized washer/dryer for church use. It'll have space-age deep-cleaning technology, and we can remote access it from the Cloud!"

Abhoc blinked. "We're talking about Sir Heckley's wife, Sir Bubo." For him, false-bragging about diddling each other's women was a sacred rite of chivalry.

"Well . . ." Bubo shifted in his seat. "She can use it, too, of course."

Abhoc reached for his sword. "Listen here, you little punk."

Heckley guffawed. "Christ's spurs! Our quartermaster here has technobabble on the brain. He doesn't care about any box unless they built it in a lab somewhere. Or any joke unless it's got *bleep blorp* in it."

Abhoc reconsidered killing Bubo. "Blorpity bleep," he growled, testing him.

"Ha ha," said Bubo, trying to smile.

"See?" said Heckley. "He thinks it's funny."

"Bloop, choo-weet!" said Bubo, flailing his arms about like a robot, laughing for sheer terror.

Abhoc nodded respectfully. "Aw, that's all right now. No harm done," he said. "But listen, I'm still going to kill you." In the moonlight, steel flashed from his scabbard.

A loud whinny startled them. At the far end of the church, a fourth mount appeared in the collapsed doorway: a monstrous destrier, almost twenty hands high, bedecked in gold barding and bearing a knight sized to match. Guided by a steady hand, the animal sidestepped the fallen lintel. Hoofbeats hammered on wooden boards strewn with stale hay and begrimed with mountain dirt windblown through broken windows.

Beneath his chin, the newcomer played a mournful fiddle. On approach, the rider paused to play to the ghosts of the congregation, who appeared fleetingly in moonlit dust swirls at the hitching posts where their mounts had stood for mass. Written for brass horns, the melody once had made heaven quake in counterpoint to the thunder of hooves upon the earth, as the Horsefolk rode hard and dauntless into the maw of British artillery. Tonight, its melancholy advance upon the midnight charger felt almost unbearably slow.

At last, Lord Brum reached the circle of torchlight in the chancel. Long blond hair fell in curls past his shoulders and upon the body of the instrument.

Letting the final note attenuate into silence, Brum leaned from his horse and hawked phlegm upon the floor.

He began to play in earnest, the famous Tartini sonata for violin.

The knights glanced amongst themselves. Though no more than an eighth Horsefolk by birth, Horace Brumfield had drunk the mare's blood mixed with his mother's milk—that's what made him one of their faith. At his coming-of-age ceremony, he had formally renounced Dodoville heterodoxies such as the Lord Jesus rode an ass and had no squire. Upon being dubbed Knight Commander, Brum had ritually bled himself with the Sacred Spur from the "ten special tender spots"—and if that didn't impress, he then pierced the two extra-painful ones nobody ever talked about. His commitment to their cause was absolute.

Yet the violin, that devil's instrument, he had not renounced *that*.

He played the sonata with dazzling speed and dexterity. The knights could hear how the music lived in his fingers, tormented his dreams, scalded streaks across the heaven of his mind like fiery comets on a clear night sky.

Brum finished. Licks of torch flame snapped in the silence.

"How I long to play that piece among the shattered bodies of our enemies."

"May you get that chance, Lord Brum," said Heckley.

"Sooner than you think, I shall." The Knight Commander regarded his men gravely. "In one month's time, we ride on Dodoville. After nearly a century, she is once again ripe for plunder."

Abhoc shivered in the cold. "She is, m'lord, but—"

"A millennium ago, our chivalrous ancestors rode in attendance on our Lord and King, Jesus Harthur the Christ. They saw his powerful right arm break the strength of our enemies; they witnessed his immortal sword, Signo, dispense justice among the faithful; they wandered with him forty days and nights through the deserts of Camelot until at last, he recaptured the holy pail from which our Chosen Steeds are branned and oated. And when they opened his side and he bled into that pail, we are the direct descendants of those who drank of that blood, heirs to the covenant which makes us rightful masters of Dodoville and all the Kolkhek mountains."

Abhoc saw no reason this should make him miss the Pharaohs game.

"We know all this for fact," he said, "as we know our own names, but—"

Brum silenced him with a glance. "You have prepared your whole lives to reclaim our marauding rights. Your skills as horsemen are unequaled. The least of you can thread a needle with your lances at a gallop. The terrible hoof-falls of your mounts at full charge make the earth itself cry for mercy. "

"Excepting none but you, my lord," said Heckley proudly, "I'd brave any man alive at the joust. But centuries have passed since the Horsefolk inspired dread in this region. Alas, what use are horses against the armored cars of the Dodoville Police?"

Brum's face, inscrutable under his mustaches, picked Heckley apart.

"Well asked," he said at last. He lifted an arm toward the shattered dome above. "This is no longer merely the abandoned place of worship of our foreriders. Welcome to the fully mechanized war stable of the New Order of Horselords. Officially open for business."

Out in the woods beyond the crumbling walls, frogs and crickets continued their night song.

"Brum, have you—?"

"Gone mad? No. I just haven't pushed the button yet."

Brum reached into his saddlebag and fished out a small remote. With a massive forefinger, he compressed the device, a hollow plastic clack. Nothing happened.

Bubo's mount, sensing her rider's apprehension, began to fret. The smaller knight patted her neck, whispering reassurance in her ear as his wide eyes surveyed the ceiling.

"Maybe put it under your chin," suggested Abhoc. "Sometimes it amplifies the signal, I dunno why."

The remote disappeared under Brum's mustaches. Somewhere, a low-decibel, high-frequency ping.

Heckley steadied his charger as the floorboards began to move.

"Sir Abhoc," shouted the Knight Commander over the rumble, "you may throw out your mount's barding if its upkeep has become a chore. Today, I have something you are going to like a lot better."

On the other side of Dodoville, snug in the rocky embrace of Mt. Myrtle, the Cumin family estate enjoyed a natural shelter from the volcano's ashen breath. On this rocky ground, the British occupiers had built Davy Castle in the nineteenth century, a basalt fortress to serve imperial administrators as a sanctuary from the local horrors—geothermal, zoological, but chiefly anthropomorphic—that plagued her majesty's holdings in the Kolkhek region, far away at the end of the earth.

After the First World War, when Dodoville got swept into the newly independent nation of Sporqia, Davy Castle remained the city's repository for learning and culture. Whatever marvels and delights were channeled in from across the globe—be they fashion, technology, or the trendiest new exercise videos—you might say they hoarded them all in there.

Atop the west spire stood the Cumin Observatory. The ash which Mt. Myrtle, one the world's largest active volcanoes, belched into the atmosphere made for an unreliable view of the cosmos. But the acoustic telescope, an engineering feat named Ladybird that peeked from the orbiting dome, pointed not skyward but down the mountain into Dodoville.

On an exercise mat by the chief observation desk, Victor Cumin divided his attention between dozens of monitors accessing closed-circuit television feeds from all over the city. He was doing burpees in a pair of running shorts and trainers.

The screens supplied views from inside police stations, the

trade floors of the Tchotchke Consortium, even the conference rooms of his own newspapers under the Cumin Media umbrella. Cutting-edge kinetophonic algorithms rapidly converted subtle motion in the video into audio reconstructions, which he could patch into by calling out the monitor's ID number.

Thanks to the digital network set in place by the Consortium's Cultural Archive Initiative, a pioneer in the field of invasive surveillance, you could now make yourself digitally present practically anywhere in Dodoville, so long as you had the resources and technological wherewithal.

For everything else, there was Ladybird here, whose audio point-and-snoop capabilities could penetrate most walls.

Squat, kick out, push up, jump! Squat, kick out, push up, jump!

Maintaining high-level cognitive function during intense physical exertion wasn't just a nice trick: for Dodoville's premier masked vigilante, it was his only chance for survival.

Plus, keeping his body in peak condition *and* monitoring criminal activity throughout the city put such constraints on his time, it really behooved him to do both at once. Afterward, he still had his ailing father's media empire to run!

Where the hell was his butler, Mori? He could at least come up here and throw swords at him or something.

"To keep your strength up, sir," said a voice.

Victor glanced back mid-squat as Mori approached with long smooth bounds, landing lightly on his bare toes. The single tail of his tuxedo rippled like a gymnast's ribbon behind his only leg. In his hands, he carried a covered silver tray.

Mori stopped beside Victor, and with a little bob at the knee, removed the lid. Vegetable soup. Not a single drop had spilled.

"Leave it on the desk there," said Victor, tucking his knees on level with Mori's eyes at the apex of his jumps.

As a skiapod, Mori moved with more speed and agility on one leg than most people could with two. Since humans had hunted skiapods like Mori across the millennia, naturally they had developed a skill for avoiding notice. Nonetheless, Victor didn't like being snuck up on in his own castle. Perception was as vital for a vigilante's survival as stealth was for the skiapod!

"Do you require my assistance, sir?" Mori smiled. Eyes the size of apples beamed at Victor beneath a broad forehead. According to Mori, skiapods had evolved childlike faces to make it difficult for less stone-hearted humans to slay them. But mostly it just creeped Victor out.

Squat, kick out, push up, jump! How many was that? Also, what was he watching on the monitors?

Oh right.

"Mori, did you know spider silk is stronger than steel? Plus, triple the blast protection of kevlar."

The butler's single eyebrow rose in surprise. "I have only a hobbyist's interest in organic chemistry, Master Victor. But yes, I did know. It's flexible too. That's why its the primary material in the Violet Storm's body armor."

"Ugh! I wear that stuff against my skin. What's the secondary material?"

"Sir, if you enjoy not getting fatally shot, stabbed, burned, bludgeoned, electrocuted, or irradiated, may I wholeheartedly suggest not insisting upon an answer to that question."

"What's grosser than spider webbing?" Victor glared at him. "Mori!"

"Skin, sir." A tilt of the head for I-told-you-so.

"Blech. At least it's not human skin."

The smile on Mori's face didn't change.

"Did you ever consider applying the silk like a shrink wrap?" Victor asked.

"I confess the thought occurred to me, sir, but I decided you were still capable of dressing yourself."

Mori's childlike face made his dry sense of humor seem slightly deranged.

"Ever think of using the spider silk on animals?" shouted Victor as he did a backflip for some reason.

"You weren't planning on riding one of the hunting terriers into combat, were you?"

"How about a horse?"

"That's a lot of spider silk."

"Where do we get ours? Do we import it?"

Mori closed his eyes for an instant. "All our silk, sir, is local. From Ariadne's Arachnophilia Euphorium."

"Emporium, you mean?"

"They are *very* enthusiastic about spiders there, sir."

11

Sweat glistened along Victor's hairline. "I wonder how an operation like that turns a profit," he said.

"It's not vigilantism in a vegetable mask, sir, but they do make a living."

Mid-burpee, Victor stopped doing burpees.

"Did you fashion my breathing apparatus out of a turnip or something?"

"No, sir. But following the specifications you gave me, well . . . Some of the writers at your newspaper have observed it looks sort of like . . ."

"What?"

"Some . . . vegetable. One of the more fear-striking ones, I presume."

Victor reached for a towel and walked over to the desk where he opened the file on the Church of the Knight Errant.

"Horace Brumfield," he said. "Named Knight Commander of the CKE three years ago. Ramped up their training programs in dressage and medieval weaponry, especially lancing."

"The Brumfields, I recall, were one of the losing families in the gang war that overthrew the Botanists from political supremacy back in the '90s."

"That's right. All their power and prestige vanished overnight. Perhaps Horace wants revenge."

Mori shrugged. "If it makes sense to a human mind, sir. Skiapods believe that dramatic reversals of fortune are simply a part of life. The rich among us cheerfully joke about the day when they will be penniless."

"Well, *of course* it'll come if they make jokes about it!"

"I don't understand, sir," Mori said smiling.

"The Horsefolk have ravaged the Kolkhek mountains since before the founding of Dodoville. They are our oldest enemy."

Mori tilted his head cheerfully. "Since the obsolescence of the war horse, the population has mostly assimilated into Dodoville society. Law-abiding, tax-paying citizens. Veterans of the Zahzian War. Nice people, if you trust reputation."

"Except the Church of the Knight Errant believes the Horsefolk will be restored to their former glory, when they ranged the Kolkhek mountains in dust-scuttling hordes, plundering and terrorizing the local population."

"Ah," said Mori. "You fear that with indestructibly-armored horses, it may actually be possible."

"Thanks to Ladybird, I know it is. I've been watching them for weeks. Weapons upgrades, elite horsemanship, a state-of-the-art saddle-mounted stereo sound system."

"A what now, sir?"

"The telescope hears the audio quality!"

"Of course."

Across his desk, Victor reached for a framed photo of himself as a boy standing beside his mother, Rochelle Cumin. He held it against his chest as he gazed off into the distance.

"The Brumfields weren't the only family hurt in that gang war. But you don't see me taking it out on the whole city."

"From a certain point of view, sir, that's exactly what—"

"I have to stop him, Mori."

13

The skiapod nodded. "Obviously, sir. He'll buy out all the silk. The way you go through bodysuits."

Victor gazed up at the battle insignia of the Violet Storm upon the wall.

"If there is any blessing in the rule of the Tchotchke Consortium," he said, "it's that Dodoville hasn't endured a full-blown gang war in twenty years. But if with these new weapons, the CKE can pose a legitimate threat to the Consortium's power . . ."

"I don't know the Knights Errant qualify as a gang, sir. They aren't political. They just want to burn things and watch people suffer."

"Sounds like politics to me."

"What do I know, sir, I'm only a skiapod. We like to make people happy! That's all politics means to us."

"And your kind is nearly extinct."

"Exactly, sir! Eradicating our foolishness from the face of the earth is the least we can do for others' comfort."

Since before Victor was born, Mori had served in the Cumin household, saying things like that with the same smile on his face. Never once had he murdered everyone in their sleep. Someday Victor would have to figure out why.

But someday would have to wait until a horde of barbarians wasn't breaking down the gate.

EPISODE TWO:

THE BAWLING AT DAGGETT BEND

"JESUS, we got enough cops?"

Officer Hammond had never seen this many faces in blue. Not even at his graduation from the academy last year.

Riding shotgun in the squad car, he cradled the coffee in his hands and let the steam warm his face. The mountain air above Dodoville was brisk at four a.m. Worse, the sleep wouldn't rub out of his eyes. He'd already put in three twelve-hour shifts this week and had been scheduled to work tomorrow when he got called up for this action.

Out on the highway, a pair of gloved hands and a shrill whistle issued directions. In the driver's seat, his partner, Clemens, waved out the window and brought the squad car around to fill out the barricade onto the road's shoulder.

Even the traffic cops are here! Hammond thought.

Up ahead he could see the domed helmets of officers in riot gear. He and Clemens had been assigned to hold the line behind them in case anything snuck through. Not bloody likely. Looked like enough to stop a tank. Let alone a few horses. Right?

"Did you forget your history book, Hammond? Can't have a repeat of last time, can we."

"That was in the 1920s. A lot has happened since then."

"Tell that to them," answered Clemens. "These folks are still living in the Middle Ages."

"The force has modernized, I mean. It's not just a bunch of us riding sideboard on some truck anymore."

"And that's why we're here. Last time, they came in on a couple hundred horses, caterwauling like a merry band. 'The British drove us out,' they said, 'but now we're back.' No welcome crew like this, and what happened? A few circuits of town, they start disrespecting old people. Breaking windows and overturning apple carts—"

"Apple carts!"

The phalanx was running drills to get the blood pumping. Instead of bludgeons, the officers were armed with four-meter anti-cavalry spears. They stood in loose formation, polycarbonate shields laid at their feet, spinning the heavy polearms above their heads in interlocking circles. Hand matched hand, boot matched boot as they executed forms with military precision. Thrusts and parries, uppercuts with the butt. A stuttered advance, striking as fast and precise as a sewing machine. Hup hup hup hup! Another spin, another flourish, and when the spears swung down into readiness at their sides, Hammond swore he heard the air shatter.

"Do a lot of damage then? Ninety years ago?"

"Would've. If they weren't so drunk they fell out the saddles."

Hammond rolled down his window. The cold air might keep him awake. "I heard the CKE has twenty-thirty animals tops," he said. "Maybe somebody should stay back in town keeping the peace."

"Rookie, in Dodoville we stay ready for horses. Maybe you heard grumbling this morning, but here's the truth: half these guys you couldn't pay time and a half to stay home. For four hundred years, this country had mad-hair hard-drinking maniacs riding bare-backed and breakneck, wineskin in one hand, jaw hammer in the other, razing houses and drinking the cream. In this town, you grow up meditating on those stories."

"You saying fellas want revenge?"

He watched Clemens take a deep breath as if exasperated this was a thing he had to explain.

"What I'm saying is, most these boys? They feel they were born a couple centuries too late."

As dawn approached, Hammond saw headlights down below, coming up around Daggett Bend. Motorcycles. Off-duty cops who hadn't gotten called up this morning. Dismounting, they clasped each other's backs in greeting and lit each other's cigarettes. Here to spectate.

One of them had a paper horse mask on a stick. Eyeholes were cut out.

"Hey, don't shoot. Bronsky. Hey, Bronsky, over here. Look at me. Guess what am I? Don't shoot."

•

Inspector Epifania Lu stood behind the barricade, watching the police helicopters patrol the airspace. For the last ten minutes, she had been trying to raise Chief Harrowfew on the comm. Worry had gnawed at her for days—something about this operation stunk. The Church of the Knight Errant had alerted them to where they'd be and when. They had promised "overwhelming force," "shock and awe," and "Dodoville come to kingdom." To believe the Horselords could rise again you had to be delusional, sure. But fifteen years in uniform, she'd developed an instinct for who was overplaying their hand. This was different. The CKE seemed a little too precise in their disorganization. Someone wanted to be underestimated.

And then a quarter hour ago, she'd gotten the email. An in-house address from a non-existent staff commandant named Orin Juglahd. Scrolling through the attachment on her tablet, everything seemed to fall into place.

"Harrowfew here," came a voice on the line, an impatient bluster. "Make it quick, Lu. This isn't your department."

"With due respect, Chief, it is. Ear to the ground, Gangland Surveillance has been hearing some weird chatter the last few days. Tall tales of every sort. The only thing consistent is today's offensive is *important*."

"CKE's not a gang, they have no political arm."

"Not yet," Lu admitted.

"Inspector, we've been watching the CKE train for months now. The riders do handstands in the saddles. Hang by the mane under the belly. Honestly, it's a good show. All sorts of circus tricks you wanna take your kid to see. But if I've got a problem, it's that I've already assigned too many resources to this operation. Just to quiet the bellyaching of those who wouldn't get to see the fireworks."

"Chief, I don't think throwing men at the problem is wise. We need to shape our tactics to the intelligence we've been receiving."

"Or counterintelligence. You sure you wanna trust what you're hearing?"

This was the part of the call Lu was dreading.

"Not just rumors, Chief. I've just received blueprints of their equestrian equipment. This is next era tech. Nothing we've seen them train with inside their hippodrome."

"Blueprints?" On the other end, the chief leaned away to issue orders to someone else. "Blueprints from whom?"

An informant who's hacking himself into the police's secret server.

"Anonymous, Chief."

More chattering on the other end.

"Maybe you're looking at theoretical horsy flying machines designed by Leonardo da Vinci."

19

Lu took a deep breath. "No, this channel has been supplying reliable intel for the last—"

"Because they're not getting past our defenses unless they are able to fly. Are you saying these horses can fly, Inspector?"

"I've had the specs less than a half hour, but . . . Thrust output versus the combined weight of animal, rider, and equipment . . ." She'd have to crunch the numbers to be sure. "From what I can tell, no."

"Good. But if these pretty pegasuses *could* fly, we have a squad of sharpshooters in the air."

"Hmh?"

"And, strictly confidentially now, a couple rocket-propelled grenades. From Hendricks' private stash."

Lu knew weapons left over from the Zahzian War were stockpiled all around town. But she was pretty sure police use of anti-tank explosives was still frowned upon. Even in Dodoville.

"Listen," she said, "I'm not suggesting we should stand down. But if this intel is reliable—and, as I said, this channel has been—" Who *were* they, though? Lu didn't like faceless informants. "We should make adjustments to our preparations."

"Which adjustments?" Harrowfew spat back the question so fast, it felt like a threat.

"The anti-cavalry unit is . . . vulnerable. I'd bring them behind the barricade. Also, thicken it by four or five cars."

"Why?"

"They jump."

"Oh, they don't fly but they jump!" The Chief did not conceal his amusement.

"The horses, yes. That is correct."

That came out more aggressive than she intended.

"All right, Inspector. Here's another thing about horses. They bleed. And they die. However many the CKE bring today, the riot line can hold twice as many. And if by some miracle . . ."

That instant when self-doubt surprises you. Lu could hear it in his silence.

"Everyone has their orders. Understood?"

"Yes, Chief." She licked her lips. "Listen, our most ancient enemy. In light of this tip-off, I justed wanted to—"

"Noted. Harrowfew out."

Official ass-covering complete, thought Lu.

The more she looked at these blueprints, the crazier they seemed. Digitial post-its proposed questions like, "How much horsepower can a powered horse power?" Playful descriptions of what individual engine modules would *sound* like. "Like an asthmatic cat wheezing in a half-empty library after eating borscht too quickly."

As if whoever sent this wanted her and only her to have the benefit of the information.

She raised her binocs and stared up at the pass where the assault was most likely to begin.

If these damn marauders didn't come down the mountain like rolling thunder, Epifania Lu was gonna feel plenty embarrassed.

•

With the morning sun crowning on the mountains, Hammond had difficulty watching the road. An hour overdue and nothing but migrating cranes coming over the peaks. He wondered if maybe the return of the Horselords was just a distraction from some other mischief in the city.

What a weird lot, them. Rumor is, once upon a time they worshiped fire. When the Order of Septic Monks brought them the gospel in the fifteenth century, the Horsefolk, despite being blood-thirsty savages, received the stories with childlike credulity. At least until they learned the savior rode an ass into glory. In indignant fury, they hunted the liarly monks nearly to extinction. The Septics, pragmatic to a fault, believed they might yet instill Christian virtue into the horseback barbarians by teaching them tales of chivalry. By some perfect storm of spite and stupidity, the Horsefolk conflated King Arthur with Jesus Christ, and the rest of this shitshow was history.

Two hours late. Well, no rumor yet of them learning to tell time.

It was felonious to bring a horse inside Dodoville city limits. Naturally: those beasts set fire to things if they stared at 'em for too long. But Hammond was part Horsefolk on his mother's side, brought up to admire their defiant free spirit. Part of him thought they deserved a chance to raze and murder in Dodoville one last time.

"I see something," he said. "Two riders. At a walk."

22

"How are they armed?"

"They look like standard bearers, sir."

"Flags?" his superior chirped over the comm.

"That's affirmative. One, the banner for the Church of the Knight Errant. The other . . . Just looks like a broom beating a cricket or something."

"A locust, I'd guess."

"Like a pestilence? A biblical plague."

"The Horsefolk are a marauding horde," someone interjected. "They don't have colors."

"Yellow blue red and green."

"What?"

"Their colors," said Hammond. "Four more riders. Bright as Chutes and Ladders pieces. Just appeared on the road behind the standard bearers."

"Give me the binocs." The voice of his sergeant on the comm. "Lancers! Well, I'll be damned. Sons a' bitches think it's medieval times."

"Looks like they are wearing . . . I dunno, some kind of spandex."

"What kind of knight wears spandex."

"The horses, sir."

"What?"

"That's who's wearing it. That's what's yellow blue red and green."

"How do you know they aren't painted?"

"Who paints a horse?"

23

"Who *spandexes* a horse?"

"Pinto," a gravelly voice suggested. "That means painted."

"Pinto means patches in the fur. It's not paint!"

"Pinto's a half-breed. White horse mated with a demon. The demon bits are red."

"They got some kind of weird tackle box on their rumps."

"That yellow one is *huge!*"

"I think those tackle boxes are engines."

"Shut up, they're going fishin'."

"Fish any closer, their heads will smart for it."

"Wish I was fishin'."

"Horses don't wear spandex. Horses don't have engines! They have scales like a dragon and their tails spin like a propeller. Don't none of you fools know science?"

"Listen, I was a machinist in the Zahzian War. I don't know what kind but that is an *engine.*"

"Yeah, so run out there and write 'em a ticket, Murph."

Laughter.

"Soon as they cross that city line, that horse will have a rope of tickets runnin' through it teeth-to-tail."

"The color guard is breaking off and turning back. The four horsemen are speeding to a trot."

"Is that the gimmick? Biblical?"

"The Four Plagues of Egypt," said a voice with awe.

An extremely loud clatter.

"Ow! What the fuck!"

"Oi! Language! I'll have your badge, Novak!"

The helicopters flew into range of the riders. "Attention. This is the police! You will not pass. Lay down your weapons."

"Such as they are," said someone at the barricade.

For a moment, they waited.

"Sounds like they're laying down some funky beats."

"They have a *stereo system?*"

"Of course. Sir Mix-a-lot was a real dude."

"God damn, I feel the earth shake from here."

"Motown. I think it's the Pointer Sisters."

"Nah. Martha and the Vandellas."

"Attention people of Dodoville! This is Knight Commander Brum of the Pestilence."

"See? See? What did I tell you? One of the plagues of Egypt!"

"*Locusts* were a plague of Egypt! Pestilence was . . ."

"Come out into the streets and set fire to your houses! And we promise you shall not be harmed!"

More silence on the comm.

"Did you know the Pointer Sisters recorded a country album?"

"You'd only have to burn a couple houses. The rest would catch on account of the wind."

"I dunno if it was a whole album. Maybe just the one song."

"Especially with them old fire codes."

"How can they name their four horsemen after *one* of the four horsemen? It's fuckin' stupid!"

"I swear to God, Novak! Language!"

"Check out the helmet that Brum is wearing. It's got bat wings on it!"

"Salt peanuts, salt peanuts!"

"Do you think Chief will let me keep that helmet?"

"It's evidence, jackass!"

"Evidence of what? Bygone Teutonic artistry?"

"Ooh, big-word Bonilla! What'd you do, go to college?"

"I learned it from your mother, Lascaux."

"But that . . . Then how come I don't know them big words, Bo?"

"Captain! They've lowered their lances! They're charging, sir!"

"Kinda far out yet, aren't they?"

"Nah, five miles' is just one Camptown race. That's how they doodah."

"BO HOW COME I DON'T KNOW THEM BIG WORDS?"

"Give me the megaphone. Attention! This is the police. Dismount your vehicles and place your hands . . . on the rumpus."

"Nice one, Captain."

"I could have worded it better, though?"

"'Put your hands *under* the hood.'"

"See, I thought that, but the joke felt a little wide right."

"Right inside the butt."

"Hey. It says 'Professionalism' on the side of the squad car."

"It says 'real cheese flavor' on the side of the box."

"Attention! This is the police. Drop your weapons and dismount, or you will be fired upon!" The captain lowered the megaphone and snapped hard to his left. "You want a write-up, Merkel?"

"I'm just sayin'! I got a cousin who puts cheese in them crackers."

They heard the hoof beats now.

"Definitely the Pointer Sisters."

"They're very excited."

"*So* excited."

"Not what you or *I* would call cheese, but."

"When I was a kid, me and my brothers used to play 'kill the horse.'"

"Still too far away."

"Sister would pretend to die from the venom bites."

"Tackle boxes! Coming on-line!"

"This goes to show. Childhood dreams do come true."

"They're barely touching the ground. Shit, how fast are they moving?"

"I told you them was fucking engines!"

The captain no longer cared about swear words. The knights activated an apparatus on their bracers and kite shields of golden light appeared on their wrists. The horses wore terrifying equine skull masks with rams' horns and frog-like goggles over the eyes. Their breath rasped over the amplification system.

Hammond heard his sergeant pacing up and down the

barricade. "Riot's got a tried-and-true anti-cavalry formation. It'll hold."

"Radar clocks 'em at 150 kph and accelerating."

"Spears or no spears," said Novak, "I wouldn't want to stand that charge."

"Sharpshooters! Take out those horses!"

"180 kph!"

"Propulsion's leaving a blue residue in the air behind them. You actually see 'em speeding up!"

By now, the police could see the riders' helmets covering their eyes and nose. Full beards were split and tied into forks. As they descended the mountain, their steeds pounded the road with hock-high metal boots that left divots in the asphalt. The knights' three-quarter riding capes flapped, fully extended behind them.

"Should we run?" mumbled a disguised voice. "I'm thinking run."

"Hold your ground!" the captain snapped. "Sharpshooters, what's the holdup?"

"No holdup, sir. Lit up the leader like a Roman candle. That spandex must be some kind of body armor. Barely slowed him down."

"220 kph!"

"A slowdown of negative forty."

"Riot unit, hold your ground! Your spearheads have nowhere to go but through."

"Neither do those lances."

"Thirty seconds."

The morning sun blinded them now, as if valkyries or avenging angels hovered behind the riders, swords drawn and trumpets blaring, which by divine grace were definitely playing the Pointer Sisters.

"Clemens? A funny time to ask, but. You ever think the worst thing about Horselords is, you never once got to see 'em live?"

"All the damn time." His partner released the safety catch on his sidearm. "It's been a privilege, Hammond."

"Yeah." A hard swallow. "Hey, Clem? I boned your wife once."

"S'ok. I love you too, man."

•

Inspector Lu watched the anti-cavalry spears snap like twigs on the horses' barding. In turn, the knights' lances pierced the face guards of the front liners—a dull pop as the tip penetrated the visor—snatching up slack bodies and tossing them like heavy sacks against the riot shields behind them. The horses trampled through after, flinging helmets and boots to rain down upon the asphalt.

As the impact threw the riot line right and left, engine flair illuminated them from behind—blinding the police like an explosion. And at the epicenter, silhouettes of four riders upon hard-galloping mounts, the enormous leader standing in the stirrups, shoulder-length curls flowing from his winged helmet, spearpoint held aloft to shatter the corona of the sun.

Watching the horses' well-muscled legs churn, Lu was not sure she saw any of their hooves actually touch the ground.

The chargers were not slowing as they approached the barricade.

The knights collapsed the shafts of their lances like a spyglass, swapping them out for a new weapon, a short pike with a thick shaft and a broad flat head. As they leveled them against the squad cars, firearms began to pop off on either side of Lu. The horsemen laid flat against their animals, vanishing behind their shields. Across the horses' chests, ripples appeared in the close-fitting armor as it dispersed the momentum of the bullets harmlessly.

"300 kph!"

Bearing down on them at the speed of thought.

"Battering rams!" Lu heard herself cry. "Move! Move!"

The pyramidal teeth of the lance-heads bore into the sides of the cars. With a crunch of metal and shattered glass, the pikes shoved the broadside of the vehicles. The off-duty motorcycle cops watched their bikes go down under the side-skidding cars, which driven by the immense collision, rolled over them and launched into the air. These improvised missiles smashed into support vehicles, toppling the operations van, pinning an ambulance, and crushing any personnel that happened to be in the way.

Having expended their momentum on this charge, the four

riders now turned and faced the line they had just plowed through. Holstering their pikes, they drew swords, hammers, and axes. The power units on the engines redirected energy to their wrist shields, which glowed vibrantly.

Someone was calling her on the comm.

"Gangland Intelligence," she barked, "Lu speaking."

"Ops just went dead, Inspector," the Chief said. "What the hell is going on?"

"The tipoff was correct. An advanced propulsion apparatus . . ."

"A jetpack. For horses."

"Essentially. Antiballistic equine armor. Module weaponry. I . . . Jesus, some kind of force field."

"What's the situation?"

"The good news is, having piled up our vehicles, the road back into Dodoville is blocked. They're trapped up here with us."

"That is not good news."

"Chief, a lot of off-duty officers here for the show this morning. We should uh . . . have the manpower to subdue just the four of them."

"That is terrible news. The road double backs under Daggett Bend. They're not trapped up there. They've cut you and half the force off from the city. You said so yourself, Inspector—"

Lu felt her heart sink. "They don't fly, they jump."

"I need those officers back in town. Pronto. Make it happen."

How did she inherit responsibility for this shitshow?

"Yes, Chief."

"Until you find someone alive who's in charge, you're in charge. Harrowfew out."

The knights made their way toward the ravine, bullets ricocheting off their mounts and shields as they hacked and slashed through the opposition, steel-encased hooves trampling those who went down before them. Their powerful arms worked tirelessly, shattering a jaw with a hammer or down-thrusting a sword behind a clavicle into the lungs and heart. Three of the knights did the brunt of the fighting, while the shield of the runtier one absorbed fire from the rear.

Some insane bacchanalia had seized the police. Ignoring the knights' onslaught, they focused their attacks upon the horses themselves, whose alien anatomies and terrifying masks held them in thrall.

In the cradle, Lu had learned what horses were, why they must be feared, why they must be destroyed. Not until she was in high school, when the entire student body had been invited up to Davy Castle for a classmate's birthday, did she learn the truth. Rochelle Cumin had shown Epifania her secret stable, full of the beautiful, docile creatures. They did not breathe fire, did not unhinge their jaws to swallow dogs alive, did not have toes like a man or a cat-o-nine-tails on their rumps. Mrs. Cumin, rest her soul, had been Zahzian, a foreigner. Ever since moving to Dodoville, she'd kept a pair of illegal mares to protect her mind from succumbing to local superstitions.

If Lu had not seen those magnificent beasts with her own

eyes that day, she probably would have still believed that monster malarkey when she woke up this morning.

But unlike horses, Dodovilleans held the Horsefolk themselves in reverence—if not because they mastered and mounted demons, then because they had always made an enemy of Dodoville's ganglord, or the British governor, or, in the long-gone days, the Council of Capricrats. And even the police had appropriated the mythos of the Horsefolk into their own identity, spiritually donning their mantle of toughness or freedom or . . . whatever. And now they faced these strange centaurs in battle, the invulnerable horses joined at the withers to their inviolate riders.

From her post, Inspector Lu could hear ribs splinter, the spurt after a carotid artery severed, the gurgle as lungs filled with blood.

The Pestilence was picking them apart.

Lu could see the knights were bare-chested beneath their capes. They were mortal under there, she assumed. She drew her sidearm and leveled it against the leader. From this angle, the laser shield allowed her access—the space between his broad shoulders target enough, even for someone who worked a desk job.

For a brief moment, she thought of Judy, her four-year-old. She thought of her growing up in Dodoville, daughter of the woman who shot the Horsefolk in the back.

Only a momentary distraction, but a moment too long.

The helicopters were now in position. A shoulder-mounted RPG appeared in the cabin door. Shit was about to get real.

On the leader's signal, all four riders turned toward the precipice. If their steeds could carry them down to the path below, the Horselords would have free rein over Dodoville. Each knight nodded his readiness. Their thrusters glowed a blinding azure as they leaped as one over the cliff.

Any officer with legs left under them ran to the edge to witness their fate. Gasps of fright escaped impoverished lungs as the bright colors drifted through mist over craggy rocks and the spearlike trunks of evergreens.

"They made it," a voice cried, not without a note of relief. As if the police had not just endured a bitter reversal, as if the city had not been left open to ruin.

Inspector Lu surveyed the carnage. A head pierced through the temple, a shoulder shattered in its socket, a knee broken the wrong way. Looking for assistance, she found a medic with a piece of fender where his eye should have been. He'd been having a smoke against the side of an ambulance when debris began to fly.

Her orders were to get the able-bodied back to defend the city, but what mattered now was helping the wounded.

Lu turned over the body of a downed officer. A sword slash to the upper thigh. The incision was deep, and without medical attention, he would bleed out.

"My only regret is . . ." The man's disconcerting pale-green irises focused on nothing. "Where were the monkeys? How much cooler if there'd been monkeys!"

Lu improvised a bandage, but it couldn't staunch the flow. She pressed on the wound with both hands and screamed for help.

"Stay with me, Clemens," she said to him.

"My whole life, all I've wanted was to see a monkey on a horse. Maybe with like . . . a flamethrower."

Her fingers were thick with blood, she was just slopping it around. She watched his face lose color. He shivered.

"Didn't you see, Clemens?" she said, holding his hand now. "Did you see what got you? It came at you with a poleaxe shaped like a candy cane. An orangutan on a Lipizzaner."

"What color?" he gasped.

What?

"The Lipizzaner. Was it white or black?"

Lipizzaners are gray, Lu thought. Or did she say it aloud? Clemens' head turned weakly from her as he muttered under his breath . . .

Did he just call her a *bitch*?

"Clemens, you must have seen it. A white stallion. White as the driven snow! Wearing a tall black plume. And—"

"A monkey on a white horse!" gasped Clemens. "Spectacular!" The spirit escaped his body in a swirl of mist.

Lu felt hot tears stain her cheeks in the cool morning air.

Was that it then? Had Dodoville just fallen on her watch?

One hope remained. The thought seemed blasphemous to

her, like the desperate prayer of a faint-hearted unbeliever. But what the Dodo PD could not do . . .

Perhaps this was work for a man in a vegetable mask.

EPISODE THREE:

LAMENT ON THE LIGHT RAIL

A LONE OFFICER stood at the police checkpoint that closed off the mountain road to civilians: all that remained between the Pestilence and Dodoville.

He had witnessed the helicopters maneuvering, heard the gunfire and the shouting. Surely, the Horsefolk were enjoying their last stand, making a heroic gesture that would cement their place in local lore forever.

Then the four riders approached, a rail of particle light pursuing them down the incline. The steeds' legs churned, steel boots throwing up asphalt like clods on a raceway. Blue yellow green and red.

And the largest of these was yellow.

Upon his giant mare, the leader road down hard upon him, long curls flouncing in the wind, the massive arm brandishing the axe above and behind his head. With the cape, it looked like the Angel of Death approaching, its wing curtained open to strike.

The bass from the saddle-mounted stereo shook the earth. The Doors. He knew before he even recognized the track.

One horse or thousands, he no longer saw. He knew his destiny was bound to this behemoth in yellow, behind its skeletal mask and the ram horns helixed like cayenne peppers past its jowls. When he heard its breath rasp like a box cutter through carpet, the prayer of entreaty died on his lips. For this was now the face of his God—the sole arbiter of his fate. He did not run. He did not hide. He didn't even try.

He closed his eyes and waited.

Hoofbeats like harbingers called:

the axe, the Axe, The Axe, The AXE.

The officer bowed his head and softly whispered: Amen!

A barehanded slap broke like a tsunami across his jaw.

The hand, course and unyielding as unsanded wood, spun him 'round and sat him down, the sting so sharp it brought tears to his eyes. At such speed, it was a wonder it had not taken his head off. As heat radiated from his face, he suddenly understood why this blow was the insufferable insult to precipitate a duel. Officer Robert Viklow, slapped. Who he was, what he was worth. The unfading outline of those heavy fingers lay upon his cheek. Now and forever.

Like a child who had received correction.

Shame. Shame.

He sat on the ground and wept for the pain, yet feeling nothing at all in his face.

•

Through! They were *through!*

For the first time since the disastrous Revelers Crusade of 1934, the Horsefolk rode into Dodoville. Abhoc let out a whoop as he stood on his saddle, his feet a flurry of belt-high kicks in a display of balance and stamina. Bubo silenced his playlist and sang acapella into the microphone: "Wanted Dead Or Alive," the traditional Horsefolk campfire song. Even Brum's grim countenance broke into a smile as he nearly beat his fellows to death with congratulatory slaps on the back.

Downtown, the morning rush had begun in earnest, congesting traffic and inciting the usual knife fights in the intersections. The agile horses moved nimbly between vehicles and pedestrians, rear-mounted jet thrusters speeding them down streets and sidewalks alike.

"Hail King Harthur!" cried the Pestilence, raising an arm in salute. "Jesus Harthur Christ is king!"

Screams of delight echoed all around them.

"Hail Arthur!" voices cried.

Thanks to Facebook, the Pestilence had ridden straight into the welcoming committee.

Anticipating the Horsefolk marauders would be slaughtered up in the mountains that morning, some whimsical individuals had made signs to celebrate the occasion and amuse those on the way to work.

"I FOR ONE WELCOME OUR NEW HORSEY OVERLORDS!" said one.

Outside the old Black Ring Security building, a banner reading "Death to the Norman" hung window to window. Below it were oversized heads of famous Normans with Xs over their eyes: Norman Rockwell, Norman Mailer, Norm McDonald, William the Conqueror, Norman Bates, Norman Reedus, Sean Connery as Richard the First, Norm from Cheers, Stormin' Norman, and Noam Chomsky, just to see who'd notice.

"Ridiculous," said Abhoc. "King Arthur fought off the Saxons, not the Normans. Even I know that."

Even he!

People in horsehead masks made archways of vuvuzelas adorned with flags. On balconies, damsels languished in some degree of feigned distress. On the street, various Merlins beat each other senseless with gnarled sticks because this is why we can't have nice things.

When the Pestilence appeared, some believed they were just part of the entertainment. Others had riled themselves up until they no longer cared.

Either way, Heckley did not intend to let down his audience. He lowered his visor and reared his horse.

"Hiho, Silverrrr!" he shouted, winning a booming cry of joy in response.

Setting his lance, he charged down the sidewalk. The tip exploded a parking meter into a cascade of coins and buttons. Igniting his booster to regain momentum, he held his aim true as he burst the rest of the machines as well, one after another like steel bubbles, all the way to the intersection.

"A cleeeean sweep," purred Bubo into the PA, fist pumping in the air. "Hoo hoo hoo hoo!"

Hoo hoo hoo hoo, said the crowd.

"Laaaadies and gentlemen," he continued, "the *finest* lancer on this *or any side* of the Antipodes . . . Sirrrrr Heckleham!"

Heckley brought his horse around toward the mess he had made. His mare put forward two forelegs and bowed deeply.

On the street, the clamor of approval shook the windows.

"They are welcoming us as liberators!" said Heckley, waving to the crowd like a beauty queen.

"Aye," said Bubo, "from their boring lives."

"Life and boredom, boredom and life," said Abhoc. He fetched a human skull from his saddlebag and held it for Heckley to see. "First one then the other, what do you say?"

Heckley glanced at Brum, who lowered his eyes in assent. Heckley beamed.

"Gentlemen and laaaa-diiiies," said Bubo into the PA, "Equessssstrian SKULL BAAAALL!"

From the roar that went up, you'd assume anybody knew what that meant.

"Mush!" yelled Abhoc, taking off at a gallop. He stood on the saddle, reins in one hand, the skull held Poor Yorick-style in

41

the other, and bowed to the crowd. Then he leaped up and heaved the skull in a high arc at the peak of his jump. He landed lightly on the horse's rump and backrolled over the saddle, scissoring its neck.

Heckley snapped the reins. "Ya!" Holding on to his pommel, he dangled off the side of his horse as it wove deftly between the midmorning traffic. Despite the height of the throw and speed of the mount, it didn't seem he would get there in time.

Like a bomb, his thruster ignited. The sound shattered the windows of nearby vehicles, a ripple of glass shards lacerating everything around it.

The horse covered a lot of ground, but the skull seemed out of reach. Heckley extended fully for the catch, sacrificing his hold and sliding from the saddle. He caught the skull lightly and flipped it back to Abhoc, who had already brought his steed galloping back the other way. Heckley caught the pommel with the toe of his boot, and he rode hands-free on the side of the horse before pulling himself back into his seat.

Abhoc bowed and stole the applause.

As he did so, the skull was snatched away by Bubo, who, before he could gloat, lost it again to Brum. Brum tossed it to Heckley, who caught it dangling off the front of his horse, holding on to the animal's neck just with his legs. He pulled himself up by its mane and laid across its back. Strike a pose! Pushing up onto one hand and one foot, he hoisted the skull aloft with his other arm.

"I call this one 'Oo de lally! Ooh la la,'" he said.

Cheers. Oh, ye gods, cheers!

Abhoc launched himself from his horse's back. Snatching the skull away from Heckley in flight, he landed across the rump of Bubo's mount. Grabbing on to Bubo's head, he used locks of hair to steer—the smaller knight acting indignant and befuddled—and guided the horse back across two lanes of traffic to run side-by-side with his own. For a moment, he stood astride the backs of both animals as their thrusters flared, galloping at ludicrous speed.

"Har-thur! Har-thur! Har-thur!" chanted the crowd, emphasizing the Lord Savior's correct middle initial.

"Boredom vanquished," said Abhoc, "I thank God."

He tossed the skull backhand over some parked cars to Brum, who let it roll across the breadth of his shoulders to his far hand, which seized it to smash a pedestrian behind the ear. When teeth flew out, it was hard to tell from which skull they emerged.

In any case, the skull had been petrified, and the young man collapsed in a dead heap.

Ooooh, said the crowd.

Brum hurled the skull back across the street to Heckley, who managed to slash a street sweeper, a delivery courier, and a custard vendor before catching it with two fingers in the eye sockets.

"Boink!" he cried, holding it up to be seen.

Ha ha ha ha, said the crowd.

"Do they think those bodies were actors?" asked Abhoc. "Or is everyone deranged? It's so hard to tell in this town."

"Enough messing around anyway," said Brum, his mustaches bristling with impatience. "We have a schedule to keep. Time to catch the light rail."

•

The Yellow Line followed the meander of the Dodos River downtown toward New Guernsey. The conductor was giving power to the train's electric motor in fits and starts. The roomy, smoke-free, low-fare cars of the light rail were already such a boon to his passengers, he didn't want to spoil them by arriving at their destinations *too* much faster than the motorists and bicyclists scrapping their way through jams on the street.

Chelsea pulled aside one of the heavy velvet curtains and pressed her face to the window. She knew something was up. Her mother wanted her to believe this was just an ordinary trip to the epigeneticist, but everything felt different. The way they didn't listen to the news this morning, the way people on the station platform were actually looking at each other—even the way the conductor stamped their tickets as they boarded had something secretive about it!

A ton of fun was out there to be had today, she thought. Every adult knew it. And they wanted to hoard it all for themselves!

A woman with red hair stood as a straphanger in the aisle.

She kept fidgeting and looking out the window. Her jaw was clenched and her fingers kept curling into a fist. Something told Chelsea if she had her way, this woman wouldn't leave a bit of good time for anybody else.

As the light rail turned into the shopping district, she saw people lining the sidewalks and standing in the windows on the upper levels. Then she spotted them: acrobats! Four men with streaming capes, leather pants, and shiny helmets who were popping handstands and turning cartwheels—all atop magical beasts! They knocked packages out of hands and stole food from people dining al fresco. Everyone applauded and cheered.

"Keep your head inside the curtain, Chelsea," her mother scolded.

But she couldn't stop looking at the animals. They really were magical, weren't they? Brightly colored as playroom toys, with steel feet that broke up the ground as they stomped. They had empty bones for heads, and—this was definitely magic—glittery bums that gave off a light of their own!

"I said don't let them see you!" Her mother was getting *very* cross.

Oh, Chelsea knew the animals were just tricks of some kind. Like when they implanted a narwhal tooth in the forehead of a goat and called it a unicorn. Just a school project, but it was still exciting, wasn't it? Life got boring with always the same animals, the same vegetables, the same epigenome. *Tedious*, she thought primly.

As the train passed, the acrobats put handkerchiefs over their noses and mouths and pulled up alongside them. They started banging on Chelsea's car with their hands. Two on each side.

"Uh oh!" cried the conductor. Arm shaking, he opened the throttle and pushed the train to more than half the legal limit.

"Look what you did," said her mother. "If you still think the doctor's going to make your eyes lilac this morning, you can forget it!"

"But Mom!" said Chelsea, pulling at her mother's hair.

She smacked the little girl's hand away. "What do we say, Chelsea? Only very bad people travel by horse."

"That's not a horse," grumbled Chelsea. "It doesn't even have fangs. It must be some kind of short-necked giraffe."

"It's a *horse*, honey. Those men just file the fangs down."

Of course, her mother was right. She recognized horses from those famous cave paintings where ancient humans rode saber-toothed tigers into battle, and the horses kicked the tigers to death and ate the men alive.

"But they wear such pretty clothes!" she said.

"They have to because their skin is worse than poison ivy."

The idea of a pretty animal she couldn't touch filled Chelsea with moral outrage.

"I don't even *get* itchy," she said.

"You will from horse hair! So don't even look at them, you'll only encourage their despicable behavior."

Chelsea watched how the animal's muscled bodies moved, how their long faces bobbed as they ran and the tails swished

46

majestically. The sound of their hooves on the asphalt was paradise.

"Mama! I want a horse for my birthday!"

"I said that's enough! I swear to God, if you are gonna act like this every time the city gets pillaged, next time we take the car."

"The car smells like cat-butt."

"You leave your brother alone! Besides, you wouldn't like horses anyway, they bite and their saliva causes necrosis. That's when—"

"I *know* what that is. It means your flesh dies and you turn into a zombie." The girl crossed her arms and pouted. "Mrs. Bowser says scientifically speaking, zombiism is absolute hoo-ha."

"Chelsea, I am your mother. I decide what's science in our house! Now, head forward, or there'll be no leek soup tonight!"

The girl faced the seat in front, defiantly watching the acrobats through the slit of the curtains. As soon as she was sixteen, she would run away from home and join the Mongols. Until then, she'd just have to learn to make her *own* leek soup. And she'd put in all the gummy worms she wanted!

While her mother was trying to see what was happening on the other side, Chelsea drew back the curtain and waved to the horses and their riders.

Her hand got smacked again.

"I said stop it!"

Ug-ghh! Chelsea hoped when the marauders boarded the

train, they'd slit everybody's throats. *That* would teach her mother to tell her what to look at.

•

The Pestilence pulled up alongside the light rail. It's stylish lines and tidy appearance turned their stomachs. Plus, it didn't smell like a stable *or* the tailpipe of a school bus. It hardly smelled like anything.

Brum banged on the side of the car. "In the name of King Harthur, I order you to stop this train!"

The light rail coasted almost to a stop. Then sped up and coasted again. Then sped up. Like some stupid kid playing with a remote control model. But mostly speeding up.

"They can't hear us, Lord Brum," said Abhoc behind him. "Sound-proof construction. The devil's work!"

"Shoulder your lances," said Brum into his radio mouthpiece. "Time to take this abomination down."

"I can hear you just fine, Lord Brum," said Heckley from the other side of the car. "This damn light rail hardly makes any noise."

Abhoc pulled the handkerchief from his face.

"It don't even cough up smoke. It's like they are begging us to rob this train."

Brum sneered. "Clean and efficient public transit will be their downfall," he said with satisfaction.

The esteemed knights and peers of the realm each took a

meter length baton from their saddle pouches. At the touch of a button, it telescoped out to three times the length with a reinforced point. They grasped the handles firmly in gloved hands.

"On my mark!" Brum cried.

"Hurry, we are almost at the station."

Up ahead the knights could see Metro workers lining the platform, ready to give the riders a stern scolding as soon as the train pulled in. Nobody on earth could natter about regulations like a DMT worker. And they were liable to issue a fine if you mouthed back!

Each rider stationed himself beside one of the wheels. The conductor, with fear in his eyes, opened the throttle until the train was going full speed. (Some of the time, anyways.)

"Steady," cried Brum. "Now!"

The knights jammed their baton in front of each of the train's wheels. The screech was horrible. The titanium rods devoured the aluminum wheels and the aluminum rails, reducing them to warped cogs and metal spaghetti. Sparks flew everywhere as the train slowed to a stop.

"Hail Harthur!" they cried in triumph.

The knights tethered their horses to the car and engaged the parking breaks. They removed their riding cloaks, folded them neatly, and laid them on the saddles. Bare-chested and smelling pleasantly of horse musk, they boarded the train.

Heckley entered first, smiling broadly under his fu manchu. "You gentlefolks weren't gonna skip our stop were you?" he said.

"Sweet Jesus," someone cried, holding their nose. "Did something die in here?"

"If you play your cards right," said Abhoc cheerfully, entering from the other side.

"Bleep bloot ter-tweet!" said Bubo, his face unreadable.

The little tech knight had been doing this ever since that altercation a month ago. Abhoc couldn't decide what this was about, but after today's pillage, he'd decide upon the correct degree of beating to administer Bubo.

Brum was walking from passenger to passenger, bending from his towering height to sniff about their heads and shoulders, his mustaches close enough to brush the skin. Some people gasped as if he had bitten them. After a moment, Brum would grunt and move onto the next.

"As Lord Jesus spake unto Gwenevere," Abhoc said, rubbing his hands together, "give unto Lancelot what is Lancelot's, but also pay your damn tithe onto me."

Heckley looked to Brum for a cue, but the giant knight was too absorbed with his huffing to give a damn.

"Don't mind that idgit," Heckley said, "he's just kidding, folks. We're not here to rob you, but to impart gentlefolkly instruction in all matters chivalrous. For instance." The knight glanced about. "Mm. You there! Why haven't you given that young lady your seat?"

Heckley pointed to a woman with red hair. The offending man wore some kind of brown bowler with a turquoise band. It was crocheted.

Abhoc pressed a hand cannon against the man's forehead. The weapon's mouth looked big enough to fire shot puts, and it was old as shit. "Don't worry, it's not loaded," he said sheepishly.

Nevertheless, he lit a match and held it close to the fuse. "But I'm going to ask you to hold still as this burns down."

"Chivalry is just patriarchy by another means," said the man in the crochet bowler.

Abhoc smiled sadly. "It could be Buick Skylark-y, but you're gonna do it today."

The man stood up angrily. "You just destroyed the rails, what good is a seat anyhow?"

Abhoc pistol-whipped him across the head. Blood spurted from above the brow as the man collapsed into the aisle. The hat rolled away across the floor of the car. It looked even more bullshit with no head in it.

"I said it wasn't loaded," Abhoc explained to the passengers, "I didn't say it wasn't heavy."

"Go ahead, ma'am," said Heckley to the woman with red hair. "Courtesy to damsels in distress, always."

"I'm not—"

Abhoc shot her a dirty look. "Going to complain? Damn right, you're not."

Something crashed onto the roof of the train. Almost politely.

"It's *him*," Bubo whispered.

Everyone listened. *Tap tap*. From where the sound originated, thin tendrils of electricity crackled along the ceiling to the corners of the car.

"Short swords, men," said Brum. "It'll be tight quarters up there."

Abhoc dumped the hand cannon into a little girl's lap. "Shoot somebody for us, would you? We haven't got time."

"I thought it wasn't loaded," the girl asked.

"Shoot your mom, then," said Abhoc. "She looks loaded to me."

The knights exited on both ends of the car. The doors clattered shut behind them.

The passengers were left alone on the train. The battered man lay unattended on the ground, bleeding badly from the head. Everybody stared at everybody.

The girl's mother whispered in her ear. "Honey, if you are going to shoot anybody, do it quickly. We are getting off."

"But Moooom, it's the Purple Onion," the girl cried, pointing to the roof. "You can tell 'cause he's wearing slippers."

"Chelsea! How do you know what slippers sound like atop a train?"

"Well, he's not wearing boots."

"Billions of non-boot wearing people on the planet and you can tell which one is up there?"

Behind the girl, a man giggled to himself. "Based on that step," he said, "I've narrowed it down to the Purple Onion or Cher, and I happen to know Cher is playing Vegas."

The girl's mom glared at that asshole. "Come along, Chelsea. Shoot this schlump with the overbite, and let's get out of here."

"Momma, it's heavy!"

"And you didn't want your physique augmented!" said the mom. "I don't understand why we even go to the epigeneticist if you are just going to be a weakling."

More footsteps now up on the roof. These were definitely the heavy riding boots of the Pestilence. The passengers listened. For a long time, nothing. Everybody up there must have been talking it over reasonably.

The man on the floor continued to bleed.

The red-haired woman let out a shriek. Mascara was running down her face like she'd been crying for days. "Today someone's gonna learn something about who's a damsel in distress!" She snatched the hand cannon from Chelsea and headed for the exit.

"It's not loaded!" called three or four voices in unison.

She grit her teeth. "It goddamn will be when I get through with him."

The cold-cocked man began to stir. "Wait, what?" he said.

•

The knights exited the car, two to the front, two to the rear. They found a set of handrails that ran up to the roof. Beside them, a gold plaque read, "Made possible by a grant from the Dodoville Council for Cinematic Violence."

The four peers scrambled up and pulled themselves nimbly onto the roof.

There he stood, like a thistle-clad god. His form-fitting onesie outlined a lean physique while a snug cowl covered his hair and ears. On the purple field of his chest, a white insignia depicted either a mountain, a flower, a cloud, a potato, or none of the above. A yellow belt buckled around his waist, and with a firm hold on the insulated grip, yellow gloves commanded a slender quarterstaff with electrified ends. Beneath his shadowy brow, a breathing mask shielded his mouth and nose.

This faceguard made a distinctly vegetal impression. Yam? Kohlrabi? A turnip perhaps.

"Good day, sirs," he said. His voice had a computerized softness, like Siri's little brother. "I am the Violet Storm."

He twirled the quarterstaff over his head, which crackled with yellow tendrils of electricity.

"We know who you are, Onion," said Brum. "We don't read the newspapers, but we do watch YouTube. And let us warn you: unlike the Archivists, our defenses are more than the people's superstitions. We Peers of the Realm are elitely trained in equestriatics, pole armisthetics, holy hand grenadiering, axemandering, swordnetics, and tripping. Plus there's four of us, so *en* fucking *garde!*"

The Purple Onion tapped the toe of his slipper on the small puncture in the roof the car.

"I want you to know," he explained serenely, "the targeter on my zipline grapple can hit this train at speeds in excess of 150 kph. I didn't have to wait for you to stop to get on."

"Sure you didn't," said Abhoc.

"Please state your names for the record," the Onion said, calm as the eye of a hurricane. "Your criminal monikers are fine. Also, if you would like to register any justification for your nefarious actions, you may do so now."

The knights looked at each other. Abhoc gestured he would like to begin the killing immediately, but Brum shoved forward Heckley, their most eloquent speaker.

"Who are we, O worthy legume," began Heckley hesitantly, "but ordinary citizens concerned with our ganglord's approach to the governance of our fair city?"

"What approach is that?" the Onion asked.

"Well," said Heckley, "the Consortium's Archive pillages the people and calls it good government. But we Pestilence pillage and . . . call it good entertainment!"

"So it's just an aesthetic quibble, then?" asked the Onion. Any intended sarcasm was lost in the computerized enunciation.

Abhoc stroked his chin. "Hadn't really thought of it like that, but yeah, that's right, I think."

"Aye!" said Heckley with enthusiasm. "You see, the Archive dresses in those phony monks' robes and appropriates your stuff. Whereas we—"

"We, on the other hand," cried Bubo, "wear *totally authentic* chivalrous accouterment."

Heckley nodded. "Passed down to us in an unbroken chain from the time and place of—"

"Of our Lord Harthur's miraculous conception at Tinkerbell Castle," said Brum austerely.

"But! What's really important," said Heckley, "is that people understand that their property, their labor, and even their very lives belong to a higher . . ."

"A feudal authority," declared Brum.

"Right," said Heckley, "We have not only the privilege—"

"Nay," exclaimed Bubo, "but the responsibility!"

"Responsibility, yes. To use said resources in an arbitrary and negligent manner."

"Which," said Abhoc grinning, "wait till you see when we get shithoused tonight!"

"But, yes, Mister Onion," concluded Heckley, "I believe you are quite correct, it's chiefly an aesthetic quibble."

The Onion slumped in disappointment. "I really expected a diatribe about getting revenge for the huge embarrassment of the Reveler's Crusade ninety years ago."

Abhoc drew back a punch at the Onion's face, but Heckley restrained it.

"Blllerrrpt-ter-woot!" said Bubo.

"What Sir Bubo means," said Heckley, "is market research shows our message plays stronger when we talk about the positive changes we can offer, instead of focusing on how we intend to raze Dodoville to the ground."

The Purple Onion lay his quarterstaff across his shoulders and scratched his head. "Could you restate the positives again?"

Bubo rolled his eyes and whistled loudly.

Heckley lay a hand reassuringly up on Bubo's shoulder. "Well," he said, "obviously people don't *want* their heads busted open. But if it should happen to their *neighbor*—"

"As undoubtedly it must happen to somebody—what, in this economy!"

"Absolutely, Sir Abhoc," said Brum. "We're promising it'll be in a public forum where *everyone* can enjoy it, not just the victim's family and closest friends."

Heckley pressed his fingertips together for rhetorical effect. "We at the Church of the Knight Errant feel *that's* a quality of life improvement, and we have the tools to accomplish it here and now."

"Aye," said Brum, indicating his sword.

"Ploot ker-floon!" twittered Bubo, beaming.

The Purple Onion spun his quarterstaff. "Gentlemen, that is some truly magnificent horse manure."

"Thanks," said Heckley, "we've been workshopping it for a while."

"The truth cannot be workshopped!" yelled the Onion calmly. "And I demand nothing less. You have enchained yourselves to the postures of your own anger, fear, and hatred. But with this staff, I will shatter those chains. With electrical shocks and ferocious bludgeoning, I shall vanquish the barrier between you and your emotional core, so that your innermost truth shall emerge in a whirlwind confession and a storm of tears!" The Onion held the staff above his head, where it flashed and thundered. "Tremble, ye mighty knights, your liberation is at hand!"

Abhoc took a swing at him before he could finish. As the Onion sidestepped, Brum thrust. The staff knocked the sword away, and the Onion's backswing caught Heckley on the hip as he leaned in to put a gladius in his back.

"Whoa," cried the Onion, "I thought you would challenge me one at a time. Where's your chivalrous single combat?"

Abhoc smiled, revealing his broken teeth. "I left it in my other pants."

The circle around him tightened.

Brum cracked his knuckles. "This time ain't nobody gonna cry when we cut up an onion."

The vigilante dragged the butt of his staff across the roof of the car, scratching up a flurry of electricity. His eyes, too, seemed to glow with a spark of their own.

"Fight me then," he said. "No more love taps."

The Onion accessed his adversaries: Eight knees in a feline crouch, four gladii glinting vows of dismemberment, one launch one flight into frenzied melee . . .

And one battle staff to confound them all!

As when a company of lumberjacks resolves to fell the tallest tree in the forest, they surround the venerable trunk in a lethal circle, bearded and dark-flanneled, and lay axes into the bark with all their vim and burl; high above, the synth-a-toned frogs, nesting birds, and far-swinging monkeys cry out in fear for home. But the obdurate heartwood of the ancient giant, having weathered countless winters and stood unwavering through century storms, does not now yield to the blows rained down upon it.

So too the Purple Onion withstood the bitter edge of the Pestilence's steel.

For a while at least. The electric twirl of the quarterstaff answered all comers, but the heavy weight of blows took their toll. Under Abhoc's assault, the Purple Onion was forced to his knees. Abhoc leaned on his sword, the unkempt scraggle of his beard one fetid breath away from the Onion's mask. The two men's eyes locked in mortal intimacy. If one had slain the other at that moment, the face of the fallen would have seared itself into the survivor's dreams, just as the vanquished would see his conqueror's face in his infernal tormentor.

Suddenly the Onion raised his head.

"Thank you, ma'am," he said, his eyes flaring to life, "but I have this under control."

Abhoc turned just in time to parry an overhand blow from an antique blunderbuss. The distressed female passenger stood over him in a red-haired rage. The gladius flew from his hand and skittered over the side of the car.

"Choo-toot burrwoing-g-g-g!" said Bubo.

"I didn't know he had a sidekick either," said Brum. "This must be the Angry Carrot."

Heckley tossed Abhoc his own hand cannon.

"This doesn't even have a *trigger*, jackass!" Abhoc called back.

Heckley smiled sheepishly. "Shucks, Sir Abhoc, I just wanted to see a gunfight atop a train today. I don't care if it's not moving. I don't even care that you have to swing it like a club. It's just . . . The heart wants what the heart wants, you know?"

"Ma'am, please return to your seat," said the Onion, "I cannot protect you in the melee area."

The woman thumped away at Abhoc, pieces of rust flying off with each blow. "I don't. Want. Your protection!"

The hand cannon was clumsy for her to swing, but even more awkward for Abhoc to parry with. It didn't help that the Onion was slapping the backs of his thighs with the prod of his staff.

The beleaguered knight turned to his companions. "Damn it, one of you pass me your sword!"

Brum scratched the back of his neck. "Mm, I'm gonna watch how this one plays out."

"Stand ye firm, Sir Abhoc," cried Heckley with hilarity, "I haveth thy back!" He thrust lazily at the Purple Onion, leaving his opponent ample opportunity to zap Abhoc.

"What do we call her?" said Bubo watching from afar. "Red Pepper?"

Brum shook his head, arms crossed over his chest. "Ragin' Radish."

Brum and Bubo knocked fists and blew it up.

While the Onion was administering a nasty shock to the back of the knight's thigh, the woman managed to catch Abhoc with an upstroke under the jaw. He collapsed like a sack of dry root vegetables.

"Shit," muttered Heckley. "Can't take you nowhere."

The red-headed woman loomed over her victim. Beads of sweat picked up eyeliner and rouge as they ran down her cheek. "And observe the goddamn speed limit when you operate a quadruped within the city!" she cried.

Heckley scooped up Abhoc and threw him from the side of the train. The body landed like bricks across the saddle, and the booster engine turned over. Heckley climbed down after to his own steed.

"This isn't settled yet, Onion," said Brum. "Take the Bratmobile up to Prismton and we'll finish this there."

"Bratmobile?" said the Purple Onion.

"That's what it's called, isn't? On account it's shaped like a sausage?"

"It's not—I am the Violet Storm!"

Brum's heavy hand clasped the Onion on the shoulder. He smiled sadly. "We all tell ourselves the truths we can live with." He somersaulted from the train car onto his mighty destrier.

"Shaped like something anyway," said Bubo, making a rude gesture with his hand and tongue. He giggled. Pinching his nose, he fell backward off the roof like a scuba diver. His blue-barded horse caught his weight effortlessly.

"Mush!" yelled Heckley.

The Purple Onion watched the exhaust of four equine engines disappear down the street.

He turned to his rescuer. Her red curls had frizzed up enormously.

"I underestimated your skills, miss. That knight was a deadly warrior. Your ability to hold your own—"

A shriek of anguish interrupted him, intense as he'd seldom heard before. And anguish was kind of his thing.

"Don't think I knocked out that piece of shit for any reason than to get to you, you pink bastard!" The firing crater of the hand cannon quivered under his chin. "You made my brother Kip cry like a *bitch*, and then you put it up on the fucking internet!"

"Me?" asked the Onion, innocently.

"Who else but you! Snot streaming into his mouth as he sobbed. About how he wished our momma was still alive!"

The Onion raised his hands above his head in truce. "So, teaming up is a no-go."

"Team up? I am *distressed*!" What had seemed like beads of sweat mussing her makeup were clearly tears. "My brother can't get no work! He's a laughing-stock. His friends don't talk to him, and he don't go out. For three months now, I haven't been able to get him off my couch! Moanin' and belly-achin' like he can't believe he ate the whole thing!"

"Kip? As in, 'Arsenic' Kip Butterman? You're his little sister?"

"Big sister!" she snobbed. "My son won't even *look* at him."

"Kip dumped outdated prescription drugs into the mixer at the baking plant, knowing it'd get sold as cupcakes to school children. Your brother is not just a criminal, he's a *very bad person*!"

"We're all bad people in this town! Some of us just have to work! Ain't no job that don't steal from someone, humiliate or bully somebody . . ."

"But children, miss. Also, how is that even a *business*?"

"Who are *you*? What do you do for a living when you're not in a full body sock? Nobody out there gets paid for *not-crimes*. So what do you *do*, Herr Jalepeño?"

The Onion shrugged. "Nothing. I'm too rich to work. So my conscience is clean, I guess."

The woman bared a mouthful of gray teeth and tried to stab him with the hand cannon.

The Purple Onion leaped softly from the train and ran to his very sausage-y car.

EPISODE FOUR:

POURING TEARS IN PRISMTON

HIGH IN THE KOLKHEK mountains, the Pestilence surveyed the city of Dodoville. Puffs of smoke from steel factories and housing fires hung like commas in the run-on sentence of its history. Under perpetual construction and conflagration, it had shrunk and expanded over the centuries, moving like an amoeba up and down the river, devouring landscape or leaving its mess behind. On any given day, the city froze over or baked in the sun, it starved or glutted, overproduced or stagnated. Always, it suffered.

Here, just below the timberline, the suburb of Prismton measured out time, the sands of every hour and year the same as the years and hours that came before. It enjoyed an ethereal existence, shrouded as often as not in clouds. The aroma of life rose from the city below, the scent of good fat burnt around the marrow-rich bone, with an acrid note of misery and ruin. It wafted into the burghers' nostrils and they were sated.

Abhoc sat upright in the saddle, a metal collar now protecting the jaw he'd injured on the light rail. It chaffed to wear, looked preposterous, and made it impossible to spit on things, but he bore it stoically.

The Pestilence had gathered outside the willow archway spanning the only road into the township. Among the wisps of bark meandered a delicate vine native to an ecosystem in the Himalayas that no longer existed. Transported to Dodoville at great expense, the exotic creeper blossomed with flowers under extensive daily care from master gardeners. The petals were tiny and green, almost like polyps.

Absolutely hideous, thought Abhoc, any way you looked at them.

"Welcome to Prissytown," growled Brum from atop his destrier. "The bejeweled buttplug of Dodoville. Down below, people bear whatever ruin we wreak with patience, for they have accepted their lot and augur nothing in it. But this place, they believe inviolate by divine decree. When we four have laid waste to their little Olympus, I swear by bright Signo they shall bend the knee and repent them of the heresy that the Lord Nazarene ever rode an ass!"

"Hail amen!" replied the rest in unison.

Bubo twisted dials and adjusted the equalizer on his sound system's control panel. "Enable your audio armor, my good sirs. These beats are gonna rock some blocks. Toot tweet!"

The four riders brushed back flowing tresses from their ears and fitted their heads with a noise-canceling helmet. In Teutonic fashion, a pair of batwings rose above the crown.

Chivalrously, the peers of the realm applied earmuffs to their horses too.

Brum, his arm braced in a leather gauntlet, raised a fist in the air.

"Ready." He glanced at Bubo, who nodded. "CHOONS!"

Bubo flipped a toggle switch. From his saddle-mounted speakers emerged a noise so aggressive, the trees themselves seemed to step back.

The riders spurred their mounts. The equo-thrusters came to life, launching the horses into a charge. The powerful musculature rippled beneath spider-silk armor as heavy hooves pounded the old cobbled road into town. The Peers rode low across the long bodies, knotting their fingers into wild manes and ululating atop the bright-colored barding: Brumish yellow followed hard by Heckley blue, Abhoc red, and Bubo green. Like a swollen river overspilling its banks, they coursed through the narrow mountain byways. The hedgerows whipped at their passing, the nets on tennis courts set a-quiver.

Mirrors in free-standing private ballet studios began to rattle. Mindfulness classes were mindful only of the god-roar of a castigating wind. In garden fountains, cherubim did spit takes. A child's pinwheel forest reversed direction.

Mommy continued to drink.

•

Arnold Fleck sat in his vesper nook, reading the *Post Repast*, the Prism's after dinner newspaper. From a bread plate, he lifted a piece of sprouted wheat sourdough toast with spreadable yak cheese and touch of honey. His glass of elderflower cordial shook pleasantly as the volcanic dome of Mt. Myrtle fulminated peacefully outside.

Until twenty years ago, he had worked as an operative during the dirtiest of Dodoville's gangland brutality and intrigue. As hard as those times had been, he still felt nostalgic for when having a bed to sleep in at night depended on whether he could eliminate his mark before sundown. In comparison, life here could seem a bit bloodless—not just the gore, of course, but the lust for excitement. Cordial and yak cheese masked only so much tedium.

Living now in this exclusive community, not a day had gone by that he hadn't felt like a trespasser. Yet he wouldn't go back for the world.

Here in Prismton, the cauldron of the city's gang wars would never bubble high enough to imperil his daughter, Morgana. She would never have to learn why Arnold screamed in his sleep or sat up nights polishing his knives in the dark by the kitchen window. She would never discover why once when she was eleven, he woke her at four a.m. and force-marched her nine kilometers into the middle of a swamp where he stopped suddenly and wailed inconsolably for half an hour. Afterward, he'd promised if she told her mother they'd had a smashing time watching the nesting ritual of the paisley-necked ibis, he would buy her an aluminum racer for her birthday. Otherwise, he'd beat her until she turned colors she never even heard of.

A racer *and* a pygmy hippopotamus, sure why not.

His glass of cordial shook more violently. This time the crystal chandelier tinkled too.

Arnold perked. That was no volcano. This could be serious.

He stood up and pressed his ear against the wall. In the distance, a deep bass sound.

No one in the Prism ever listened to music over a conversational level. Even when a string quartet performed at your society event, one always kept them a few rooms removed from where guests were gathered. You instructed them to play the lesser works of minor composers, so as not to spoil the evening by making someone feel anything.

He could make it out now. "Ghost Riders in the Sky." A remix of the 1998 duet track with Willie Nelson. It was loud.

A gangland invasion. However improbable, no other explanation existed.

Calmly, Arnold Fleck folded his newspaper and laid it on the table. He unbuttoned his shirt and hung it neatly on the back of his chair. Strolling down the hall, he stepped into to a small room with no obvious purpose. From a secret compartment above the dummy fireplace, he removed a sweet-smelling bottle, from which he applied oil to his arms and chest until the flesh glistened. Next, he reinforced both wrists with a roll of tape. To his body, he strapped a pair of throwing axes.

Getting down on one knee, he screwed together the two halves of his three-meter footman's pike. He performed this ritual the same way he prepared his cue for an afternoon game of snooker with his neighbor, Hals Crick. Both men preferred snooker to billiards because it was joyless to watch and even less fun to play.

In his hands, Arnold tested the balance of the polearm. As he gazed down the shaft, he thought of the length of years that had past since he last engaged in street combat. He wondered if his muscles remembered the gestures of war, if they could still perform with precision.

Years ago, when he had smuggled this weaponry into his home under cover of darkness, he had been thinking about the defense of his property and the safety of his family. None of that entered his mind now. The music that came booming down the road had awoken some long-forgotten corner of his psyche. Either he would vanquish his enemies today and bathe his limbs in their blood, or he himself would be slain at their hands. It hardly mattered which, the fight itself was the thing. The stink of engagement, the blood and sweat and shit and screaming!

Amen, something cried aloud in his soul. *Sweet God, amen.*

Having thus invoked the witness of heaven, he snuck out the servant's door, in pursuit of the raucous sound.

He wasn't prepared for jet-powered horses. He simply wasn't.

On the other hand, the Pestilence wasn't prepared for Arnold Fleck.

•

The knights jetted along the mountain roads, trailing streaks of light behind them liked bright-colored snakes from an old-fashioned arcade game: yellow red blue and green. From the palatial houses looming above the roadside hedges, the air itself seemed to ripple as they passed, specks of residue sparkling in their wake.

Just as clouds envelop the highest peaks, so too the nightmarish riders clung like a mist to Mt. Myrtle, thick and churning upon her crags. They shook the earth with the thunder of hooves, the combustion of engines, the unrelenting bludgeoning of subwoofers.

Once, twice they raised dust on the pathways, three times to announce their business. This task completed, the Pestilence powered down their steeds and drew them up in the town square. Bubo Skymole cut the music.

In the center of the plaza stood a glass pyramid, the eponymous installation which semiannually, upon the vernal and autumnal equinoxes, fragmented the sun into seven distinctly-colored lances of light, each striking and illuminating one of seven crystal statues that stood about the plaza in a circle, exquisitely crafted anthropomorphic representations of the seven cardinal virtues.

Which are: Temperance, Fortitude . . . Cleanliness? Who the hell knows.

Every March, and then again in September, school children were carted up from Dodoville in sticky busloads to witness the miraculous event. The town council sent out a lavish cheese plate and informed the children that the Prismites had very much desired to greet them, but unfortunately, everyone had planned other engagements months before the movement of the sun had been scheduled.

From his saddle, Abhoc swung a hammer at the head of (what may well have been) Patience. It shattered into a thousand pricks of glittering light.

Brum spoke. "Eyes about you. That romp through town ought to draw out their security personnel. Better to fight them here than to challenge them door-to-door."

They waited.

Gradually, shadows began darting between the columns of the porticoes at the edge of the square.

A landscaper with garden shears. A charwoman with a washing board and wooden pail. Abhoc could barely make them out. But he had been in the face-mashing business long enough to notice when someone was forming a perimeter.

"Surely not those lot?" he said quietly.

"Aye," said Brum. "Don't underestimate them. Their household tools will be optimally weighted for lethal force."

The washerwoman began to twirl her bucket over her head

and about her shoulders. The motion struck Abhoc as . . . nunchuck-ish.

"Seriously?" he said.

Abhoc turned to see a tailor approaching on his flank. By size and stature, the man looked like a fifty-year-old schoolboy. Impeccably crisp creases dropped from just above his inseam, and his shoes were polished to a razor shine. He removed a tape measure from around his neck and wrapped it twice around his knuckles. The dark curly arm hair below three-quarter-rolled cuffs bespoke a quiet dominance.

"The deadliest warriors you'll encounter today," observed Brum, "top graduates from the most prestigious schools of domestic ergomachy in the world."

"What's . . ."

"Like, butler kung fu."

"I refuse to believe that's real," said Heckley.

"Wait till you get a serving fork in the throat then! Prissytown believes it's uncouth for guards to patrol here, so they disguise them among the help. Plus, having them beat out carpets saves on wages."

A man in tiny shorts and sweatbands stepped out from behind the glittering statue of Fiscal Responsibility.

"Is that tennis instructor really going to come after us with his racket?"

Brum soothed his steed against the gasoline scent of an approaching auto mechanic.

"Aye. Power up your laser bucklers," he said. "His balls will conceal edged weapons or combustibles."

The smaller green knight was keying the touch screen on his saddle console.

"*En garde*, Sir Bubo!" shouted Heckley. "The charwoman behind you is gonna scrub those freckles right off your nose."

Beep bop boop beet toot tweet! went Bubo's display. Furiously, his fingers continued to type and swipe.

"Hold them off a few," he said. "I'm searching my armory databases for tactical weaknesses in the local combat liveries."

"Smart thinking," Heckley conceded.

"Two masseurs and a dog walker," shouted Brum, "four o'clock."

"Afraid of nothing, me," said Abhoc, gnawing his lip. "But I don't even wanna know what that wet nurse is going to try."

Heckley spat on the ground. "Yeah, you do. You sir freak."

From one of the roads that emptied into the plaza stepped a man in linen slacks. His body was vested with standard melee weapons and he didn't seem to have come from any domestic task at all.

"Who the fuck is Rambo over there?" asked Abhoc.

Noticing eyes upon him, the man brandished a pike the length of two men. The end shone with a diamond glint.

Brum's horse whinnied as he turned it sharply in the newcomer's direction. "That, sir knight, will be the master of the house. We take that one alive. For ransom."

The pikeman assumed a battle stance.

"If that's a diamond tip," said Heckley, "do you think it could pierce your mount's barding?"

"God give him the courage to find out." Brum set his teeth and spurred his charger. The massive horse accelerated under its own power as the lance aimed for its quarry's heart.

"I don't see how that is going to keep him very alive," Abhoc said to Heckley.

The blue knight chuckled. "You'd be amazed what a body can ransom for. We do it at the Archive all the time."

Abhoc shrugged. "Maybe I'm just not sentimental," he said, "but if it can't chat nor eat toast no more, I don't want it."

Brum lowered his visor.

The pikeman beheld a yellow demon with two heads and six limbs, snorting and sparking the ground with its hoof falls as it bore down upon him. His feet shuffled upon the flagstones.

For an instant, the flash of a smile crossed his face.

Then he turned and ran, the pike clattering on the ground behind him.

•

Breathing heavily and covered in sweet, Arnold Fleck reached his eight-car garage. After all these years without killing a man with his hands, it seemed a pity to retreat from those knights in the plaza, but he'd simply had no choice.

The opportunity was too big to turn down.

Opening the garage door, Arnold beheld the Duesenberg

roadster he was supposed to be working on. You couldn't smell a drop of oil in here. Every few months he would order a new part to replace one he had moved to a museum case on the wall. Hals Crick would come over and look between the car and the part. Arnold would say where the part was purchased, whether he'd needed it custom made, how much trouble it had cost him to have it shipped up here on Mt. Myrtle. Hals Crick would look between the part and the car. Cloths were removed, cloths were replaced. Otherwise, nobody touched anything. The ritual took over an hour.

Arnold's involvement with Dodoville gangs began at the tender age of eleven. His first job had been to euthanize the wounded after a street fight and collect their valuables for his ganglord's war chest. Later, as he took on more dangerous work, fellow operatives encouraged him to spend his share of the spoils on fast pleasures. In this business, you never thought past the next job or the next orgiastic all-night celebration. But Arnold found that left you with empty pockets in the morning, overeager to accept the next desperate job. Wouldn't he live longer if he thought about his future?

A keen observer, Arnold developed a knack for anticipating the outplay of gangland power struggles. Over his tenure, the balance of power in the underworld shifted drastically three times. Three times he had changed allegiances at the ideal moment. He had functioned as a key operative in the rise of the theater empire of Rhadamanthus Flynn, of Dr. Cynthia Pack and her botanists, and finally of Jaxon Stahler's Consortium.

Then he pocketed his earnings. Gangland respected the canny renegotiation of loyalties, but to squirrel away the rewards of valor was too highbrow for a lowlife. Each organization had valued his knowledge and experience, but they always considered him a stale breath in the room.

Duesenberg. Even the word sounded like a slow death by dysentery.

Arnold got used to being disliked by his peers. When he finally wanted out, no one was sorry to see him go. Up on the mountain with you, they said. Where old oracles belong.

Now he performed everything in his life with a bloodless boring decorum. When he was finished, he double checked to make sure it was boring and bloodless enough. Over his many years of cheating death, Arnold never imagined the payoff would be pretending to work on classic cars—yet he wasn't sure why he should have expected anything else.

Sometimes at night, he thought back on the magnificent bastards he had outsmarted and outlived. Now they were getting their revenge, he thought.

Well, until today. Today the sanctity of his hearth and home was under attack from savage horseback marauders. Today belonged to him.

Crated away behind the half-empty shell of the Duesenberg was Arnold's real project, a fully functional gasoline-powered ballista whose meticulous upkeep and ongoing improvements was his life's only joy. He called it the Queequeg. A classical machinist in Winnipeg had designed it be the most deadly accurate anti-horse spear cannon this or any side of the Middle Ages. With a twenty-first-century digital targeting system, the specs claimed it could drive a 2.5m ashwood projectile through the eye of a racehorse at full gallop. The titanium alloy spearheads were guaranteed to stick in the side of a tank.

Unboxing the Queequeg with the enemy outside, Arnold felt like a bridegroom before his virgin bride. He unbuckled the knife belt from his waist and let it fall to the floor. Pulling himself up into the operator's seat, he allowed the suspension spindle to adjust to his weight. As his hand wrapped around the custom steering apparatus, fitting his thumb into the divot of the launch button, he gasped involuntarily. With a half key turn, the engine turned over and purred. Arnold shifted a handle, causing the tension mechanism to draw back and lock into place with a satisfying click. A bolt dropped into the firing groove from the side-mounted quiver. The targeting system responded to the lightest pressure from his hand, directing the bolt with a motor-assisted swivel that shifted the seat beneath him, keeping his eye aligned with the crosshairs.

Arnold Fleck fell into a reverie. The old battles, the narrow escapes, his enemies' delicious screams of agony and fear.

In his day, he had butchered aluminum workers, theater ushers, botanists, tchotchke salesmen—the most vicious gang operatives Dodoville had ever seen. But one thing had always been missing from his life, one enemy he had never confronted: the Horselords, the Kolkhek region's primeval threat. Now he could almost smell the stink of their perspiration.

As a boy he had daydreamed about living in the fifteenth century, the hoofbeats rolling off the mountain in waves of terror, himself standing in a doorway, ready to gut them all with a stove poker or whatever.

Fifty years of fantasy. Today he would fight them. Live or die, he would finally be whole.

On his cell phone, he dialed Anne's number.

"Honey, I need you to roll out the extra ammo cart onto the driveway."

"Are you mad? What cart?"

"For the Queequeg. The Horselords are here."

"What, for dinner? Listen, Feefo, I can't play right now. Kathrine Lady Corner-of-Essex-and-Marsh is showing me the new dresses she bought her Pekingese."

"The Horselords are *attacking*." With relish, he licked his lips. *"Just like we always dreamed."*

A strangled gurgle on the other end. He heard the phone fall to the ground. A dog yapped in fear and rage.

"Anne?"

A distant piercing cry.

"Anne! Are you all right? Anne!"

"Don't kill them all till I get there," she said.

Arnold forbade the love to enter his voice. "There's only four. Get moving quick."

•

Back in the town plaza, the Pestilence had their hands full.

As knight commander, Brum could not leave the field, so Heckley lowered his lance and charged after the fleeing pikeman. With a good pick, he could slide the point under the leather straps across his chest and haul him off the ground. If he missed low, he'd spear him through the shoulder. Just as good.

The landscaper, however, caught Heckley's lance in his gardening sheers, jamming the weapon in his hands. With a powerful wrench, he twisted the rider off balance and pulled him from his horse. Heckley hit the ground at a roll, bouncing back up to his feet. He swore bitterly as he watched Arnold Fleck make an escape.

The tailor addressed Abhoc, snapping the tape ruler wrapped around his fists. "Face me," he said, "if you think you measure up."

Abhoc twirled the axe in his hands. "Puns? Is that your special power? Gonna leave me *in stitches?*"

The tailor smiled wryly. "Look at you, m'lord," he said. "presenting yourself like a barbarian. To succeed as a knight, you must dress as a knight, conveying chivalry down to the smallest detail of your attire. Otherwise . . ."

The small man flicked his measuring tape like a whip. The metal tip struck Abhoc so sharply on the nipple, the knight screamed in his saddle. The horse, too, reared at the sudden crack and turned to bolt.

Abhoc regained control of his mount and gave it his spur. Vanquishing the distance between them, he grabbed the tailor by the shirt and hoisted him up.

As his feet left the ground, the tailor spat out a pair of sewing pins from between his teeth and stabbed them together into Abhoc's wrist, all the way down to the heads. With a flurry of movement as crisp as his creases, he broke free of the hold and landed softly.

Abhoc grunted as he pulled out the needles with his teeth, then brought his horse around again. "Don't make this personal, old man. You may be crafty, but you are just the tailor!"

"Sew I seams!"

The tailor removed his vest and held it in front of him like a matador. He motioned for the knight to bring it.

Meanwhile, on the other side of the prism, the tennis instructor whistled for Brum's attention. The knight turned to see him on the balls of his feet, shoulder width apart. He held the racket in front of him, as if awaiting a volley.

"Combustion shield!" Brum cried. A kite-shaped plane of light appeared on his wrist guard. Holding it in front of his face, he set his lance and charged.

Brum totally got served.

The instructor raised the racket above his head and drove a peach-sized sphere toward Brum with an overhand smash. It whistled through the air and exploded against the barrier of light with enough concussion to drive his mount back and break its stride.

"You'll get no love from me," said the instructor with a wicked grin.

"Jesus Harthur Christ," Brum cried, clenching his chest in agony. "You just lobbed a bomb at me, but *that* was painful."

The instructor bent at the knees and readied himself for another volley. Brum lowered his lance and aimed for the heart. His opponent awaited the charge with nerves of steel.

At the last instant, the instructor hopped lightly to one side and brought the racket around in a backhand slice. A metal plating on the rear of the racket made brutal contact with the head of the lance, releasing a shower of sparks and bending the tip.

"Break point," said the instructor dryly.

"Listen here, saucy! I've some tennis for you too."

Brum drew his war hammer, an ugly thing heeled with a vicious spike. With an off-hand blow, Brum caught his opponent heavily on the back of the skull, dropping him to the ground as his head broke open like a ripe melon. The instructor lay there in a puddle of blood and bone.

"It's called sudden death," he said.

•

"Stiletto" Anne Fleck had never worn a heel over an inch and a half in her life: a thing you oughta know before you cross her.

Before their marriage, she and Arnold had partnered on dozens of gangland jobs. Undercover as a quarreling couple, they constituted one the most ruthlessly efficient assassin teams Dodoville had ever seen. They anticipated each other's actions and behaved as a single organism, able to salvage a well-laid plan gone sour or to disappear a witness who wasn't supposed to be there.

When Arnold decided to reinvent himself as a member of Dodoville's suburban leisure class, Anne was the obvious co-conspirator. The money was a small matter. Forging the ancient lineages, the trusted connections, that unfakeable above-it-allness, even that was manageable. But working opposite ends of the room in tandem took something special. By dividing, they conquered. Arnold and Anne: the Flecks. Their deepest covert op yet.

The transition to domestic life did not provide the peace and quiet they had hoped for. The Prism, too, they found very much a war, only now the trenches stretched through rose gardens and piano recitals. The same arguments which they had once shammed in public now lost their flavor in the privacy of their new home. Neither could stand the same foods or movies as the other. The scent of the hand soap proved a minefield.

Sexual compatibility, let's don't even talk.

The most treacherous thing of all: the dysfunctionality of their marriage proved the most convincing part of their cover.

The pool of eligible partners for Prismites was small, and since they seemed to cultivate themselves as people of few qualities, building an emotionally supportive partnership was sort of a lost cause. Profound spiritual isolation was simply the fee you paid to live above the fracas of Dodoville.

In every parlor and smoking lounge, the laughter was forced or nervous. Whenever you looked at a lawn, either yours or a neighbor's, you were scanning for weeds. A dinner party was deemed a success if everyone had been made too anesthetized to complain.

Dinner was always a success.

Of course, the Flecks hated each other. Of course, each was waiting for the other to die. Otherwise, people would have smelled something fishy.

Anne was waifish, like most Prism wives. Naturally petite, the slight figure was not difficult for her to maintain, but sometimes she starved herself anyway, as recreation. Hypoglycemia spiced up an otherwise insufferable day.

After living here a few months, she resolved that someday she would execute everyone in town—one at a time as the lights went out, like some campy whodunit. But as the years passed, she decided she could wish no greater evil upon her neighbors than to leave them in their state of restless paralysis. It's what she would do if she was exacting revenge upon herself.

Finally, she realized everyone else thought of themselves as letting *her* live. The peace here was spite-based. It had always had been.

Today, Anne had spent the morning having her hair processed until you could no longer say whether or not it had a color. Her tea dress, Christmas red, cost as much as a small ship. It cinched just below her armpits and hung in a way that obliterated any sense of physical form. Like the robe of a Dickensian ghost, it could be hiding anything under there: a desert oasis; a Tony Award-winning musical; a cloud-swirling portal to Narnia. With a pair of blocky shoes at the bottom.

She stared at herself in the mirror. She looked like an overused shuttlecock.

With a sewing needle, she drew a drop of blood from her finger and smeared it across her forehead. With the back of her hand, she wiped her lipstick across her cheek in the other direction.

As she slipped a stiletto into the belt of her dress, an electric charge flooded her body. She felt like an old computer coming back online.

Snarling at herself in the mirror, she ran the flat of her tongue across her reflection in the glass. The mousy Prismite she'd been this morning lay in a trunk somewhere, buried under last season's fashions. This was the real her. Stiletto Anne, dressed for war.

·

The Pestilence was hard at work. With laser lassos and turbo thrusters, they pulled down obelisks of priceless crystal and watched them shatter across the stones of the plaza. The pieces lay in pools of massage oil and toilet cleaner, spilled by the domestic defenders now routed and retreating into the shadows of the surrounding porticoes.

Time and again, stories of heroes have taught us that however much courage and tenacity you bring to the battlefield, no weapon is more powerful than a good pedigree. The Prism domestics had fought fiercely but ultimately proved no match for the Pestilence, who'd had the foresight to grant themselves noble titles, on account the houses they came from were technically very old.

Also, the servants had been forced to fight with like a waffle iron, so who knows.

When vandalism started to bore them, Brum drew up his knights in a line.

"Valiant sirs," he said, "have a look on yonder hill. You could not say any of those ugly fucking houses to be uglier or fuckier than the rest. Prissytown has a byzantine set of building codes to make sure every home falls in line with some dead lunatic's concept of what Vienna under Emperor Leopold the Somethingth might have looked like."

"So what is our strategy?" asked Heckley.

"We must strike them where it hurts most," said Brum.

"The groin?" suggested Abhoc.

"The lawns."

"That's what I meant. Loins."

A late afternoon wind whistled over his balding head, splaying strands behind him.

"Sir Abhoc, beat yourself twice in the face," said Brum.

The red cavalier made a fist, then paused.

"It's already very badly bruised, Knight Commander."

"Three times."

Abhoc administered the punishment, swearing profusely with each punch.

"Sir Bubo!" cried Brum. "You know your duty."

"Yes, Lord Commander. Say no more."

The leather-goggled knight of the realm attached one end of a hose to a tank on the side of his horse, the other to the butt of his lance. On the handle, he toggled a switch from STABBY to FLAMETHROWER.

"Ever since a botanist killed my uncle," said Bubo, "all I yearn for nightly is a world without privets."

"See," cried Abhoc, pointing indignantly, "he's calling 'em groins too!"

Brum cast him a dark look. Abhoc instinctively covered his swollen jaw.

"A *privet*," Brum explained calmly, "is those hedges lining the estates here."

"Oh, I see. On account it's privet property and all."

"Good Lord on a Lipizzaner!" cried Heckley. "The boss was giving you a chance!"

"How many lives has a cat, Sir Abhoc?" asked Brum.

"Nine," he replied.

"And how many tails?"

"Just the . . ." Abhoc's face sunk. "You're having me whipped again after this, aren't you, m'lord?"

Brum scowled. "Don't give me ideas."

A jet of black-tinged fire spat from the tip of Bubo's lance. Spurring his mount, he passed down the road at a light trot, applying the burning edge of the flame to the bushes on one side. Where a tree overhung the shrubbery, he paused to drench it with dollops of sticky fire. His horse shied as the flames shot up, but Bubo patted its neck and whispered soothing clicks in its ear. Once the animal had steadied again, the two worked on till the bend in the road. Then the knight lowered his lance and made a pass back along the other side.

The road had become a corridor of flame, towering four meters high.

"This is exactly what my dreams are like every night," mused Abhoc, rubbing the smoke from eyes.

Up ahead, a long automobile rolled out onto the gravel path. It came to a full stop and turned on its headlights, flooding the burning passage with an eerie lavender glow. The engine revved like the world was coming to an end, then softened to a purr.

The Bratmobile. Flanked by an inferno on each side, it was truly a terror to behold.

On the driver's side, a long metal pike rolled off the roof to settle onto a pair of bracing arms. At the end of the pike, a red targeting light winked at the knights.

A yellow glove on a purple wrist reached out the window and beckoned.

"Does he want us to tourney with his car?" Abhoc asked incredulously.

Heckley crossed his arms. "For all I know, he expects us to wash his windshield."

An unsettlingly tranquil voice emerged from a loudspeaker. "I, the Violet Storm of Dodoville, challenge your champion to a contest of arms, in the solemn rite of the joust!"

The knights glanced at each other. "Is that even fair?" asked Abhoc.

Heckley lifted his helmet to scratch behind his ear. "On a pass of lances, I'd rather have my horse than his car. Isn't that right, Sir Bubo?"

"I dunno, let me ask. *Tweet toot twerp tawhit,*" he said into his saddle console.

Slowly rotating digital diagrams of both the Bratmobile and the Pestilence's equo-gear lit up with point-by-point comparison analytics.

"That witchy box understands him!" remarked Abhoc.

"With this build," said Bubo, studying the screen, "you should have slightly better odds for survival in a head-on collision. Although . . ."

Heckley trotted out into the road. "Hey Artichoke! If you wanna joust, you have to sit on top of something. Those are the rules!"

As if anticipating this, the Purple Onion climbed out a window and scrambled up on the roof with a rope in his hand. Leaning over the side, he pulled up another rope from the opposite window. As he tugged on one end then the other, the front wheels of the Bratmobile turned left and then right.

Abhoc nodded toward the rope-steering mechanism. "Hey Heck, you think I should try that sometime?"

Heckley laughed. "Could only really improve your driving, Sir Abhoc," he said.

Straddling the car, the Purple Onion hefted the makeshift lance in his right hand. A trapdoor opened atop the roof and locked in place to serve as a shield. It was emblazoned with the Violet Storm insignia.

"That configuration does *not* meet league regulations for motor-powered mounts," observed Bubo.

Heckley shrugged. "Remind me to file a complaint with the tournament board after I kill him." He lowered his infrared lance-guider goggles over his eyes and ignited his light shield.

"Stand down, Sir Heckleham," said Brum. "I got this."

Heckley trotted to the shoulder of the road and let Brum take his place.

The sound of the steed's engine coming online sounded like a fighter plane preparing for takeoff.

"To the winner of the joust goes Prissytown," spoke Brum into his headpiece, the voice amplified over his horse's saddle speaker.

"And the loser," replied the Purple Onion, "will make a full confession of his crimes and inadequacies amid wailing and gnashing of teeth!"

Brum shrugged. "Suit yourself," he said.

"Agree or disagree," said the Onion's computerized voice.

"Agree," said Brum, impatiently. "Sir Bubo! Ready my autolance!"

(This was a lance for skewering automobiles, not a lance that operated by itself. Confusing, unfortunately, but no one is going to say "carlance.")

It was the largest, thickest jousting ram ever made. Veins of computer light ran the length of the shaft, and it was front-loaded with a four-finned head designed for brutal penetrating power.

"Abhoc!" cried Brum. "Make yourself useful. Trot out halfway between us and be ready to drop your lace hanky."

"It's not lace, it's just a hanky," sneered Abhoc, but going all the same.

"Dismount," called Heckley. "And don't just stand there, look pretty!"

The Purple Onion flashed his headlights in the smoke, and the engine revved. Dash controls seemed to have been installed on the trapdoor panel.

Brum shifted the gear stick on his horse into neutral then flung it into first. The tail thruster began to glow, and the air around it could be seen to bend and ripple.

Abhoc waited on the side of the road with his handkerchief raised above his head. It wasn't lace but it was definitely embroidered.

Heckley whistled. "Show us some leg, you sexy thing!"

"You'll see more than you can handle if you don't shut your hay hole!"

The Purple Onion tapped the roof of his car twice to show he was ready. "Your ride of terror ends here, Pestilence."

"You want my tears, Onion," cried Brum, "come and claim them!"

Heckley, miffed at his knight commander for benching him in the lance games, displaced his anger at the Onion. "What makes you think you can hold your own against the greatest jouster of the End Ages?" he asked.

"Horace Skelton Brumfield is only a man," replied the Onion.

"And what are you, freak?"

The Bratmobile's engine revved in response.

Brum nodded to Abhoc, who dropped the handkerchief.

The car leaped into motion. The Purple Onion straddled the roof, holding the reins to the steering wheel in one hand. In the other, he gripped the lance in his glove. Brum spurred his horse into a light trot. With quarter the distance between them covered, he lowered the lance and the horse began to run. At half distance, the booster kicked in and his steed disappeared into an equine blur, his lance's computer light racing in pulses down the length of the shaft.

Both pairs of eyes locked firmly upon their opponent's shield.

Neither saw the ballista missile strike Brum's horse just behind the shoulder.

The spider silk armor deflected the bolt, but the momentum knocked the animal around sideways. Brum's mare whinnied in dismay as her booster's propulsion veered her helplessly into the path of the Bratmobile. The Purple Onion, steering by some kind of pulley system, yanked sharply on the reins to avoid a high-speed collision with the enormous horse. The car disappeared through the flaming hedges.

"Yussss!" Arnold Fleck shouted, his voice ghostly in the thin mountain air. "Got him. Right in the goddamn horse!"

Either due to the roof control panel being thrashed with foliage or because it was now drenched in liquid flame—or maybe because not even a superhero can find the right button while careening atop an automobile—the breaks never activated. The Bratmobile sped up a ramp into a gazebo, launched over the front garden, smashed through a bay window, and careened through several of the manor's more expensive rooms.

Finally thrown clear of the roof, the Onion's lance embedded itself in a free-standing replica of the Venus de Milo in the marble foyer. The angular momentum spun him head-over-heels around the handle several times before he made a clean dismount.

When the world stopped spinning, the Onion glanced up at the statue. The lance had pierced Venus right through the heart, as cleanly as if Cupid himself had fired an arrow.

Nice shot, he thought.

•

Hals Crick shuffled through the house in his smoking jacket and slippers. He'd been puffing serenely on a pipe in the west parlor when he'd heard the Johnny Cash roaming the backroads. Once the roaring flames started to consume the foliage out front, he got up to change the phonograph. Finally, when it sounded like a bomb had torn through the Fleck manor next door, he felt compelled to step outside and investigate.

It's rather pleasant out, he thought, as he stepped onto the veranda.

Through the rails of the front gate, the blur of a half-naked man ran past screaming. He was wearing a metal cone on his neck, like the kind that keeps dogs from gnawing at a bandage.

"Help!" he cried. "Some crazy munchkin lady is trying to stab me! With a shoe! With a shooooe!"

Hals took a long draw on his pipe. "Don't be Anne don't be Anne don't be Anne."

A few seconds later, he saw Mrs. Fleck charge after the knight, wielding a yellow pump with a knife for a heel. Her hair was a little bit on fire.

Hals sighed. "I better get the good cognac," he said as he disappeared back in the house.

•

The Flecks' vesper nook wasn't large enough for six men. But the Bratmobile had destroyed the dining hall, the breakfast nook, the second dining hall, the snacking atrium, the parlor refreshment kiosk, and the eating room. The Purple Onion sat at one end of the table, Arnold Fleck on the other, with the four members of the Pestilence taking up the side benches. You couldn't fit an elbow anywhere, but despite the cramping, everyone was very polite and made an effort to appear to be having a good time.

"Can I offer anybody more tea?" asked Anne.

"No thank you, Mrs. Fleck," said Brum, "you've already done so much."

"I would have had a nicer spread prepared," she said, "but I don't know where Lacey has gone. She was here about an hour ago . . ."

"About this high?" said Abhoc, raising a hand to his chin, "short hair, charming little mole below her lip?"

"Yes, that's her, Mr. Abhoc. Have you seen her?"

Abhoc snickered as he glanced at Heckley. The blue knight elbowed him in the ribs.

"I'm sorry, Mrs. Fleck," said Heckley. "You have been so kind. I'm afraid she . . . won't be coming back. I hope that's not an inconvenience?"

Crestfallen, Anne tried to smile. "Oh, not at all, not at all! I was going to fire her anyway. It's so hard to get a girl who can crust a sandwich correctly. You've done me a favor really, I just . . ."

Anne burst into tears as she ran out of the room.

Heckley frowned toward Arnold Fleck. "Should some-body . . . ?"

Arnold shook his head. "No, don't think about it. It's all the soot in the air. Her eyes water whenever the volcano acts up like this."

The Purple Onion, wearing a mask over his mouth and nose, lifted his cup with a pinky raised, then set it down again. "Let me try, Mr. Fleck. Managing manifestations of emotion like this is kind of my thing."

"Not at all!" protested Arnold. "Please, you are a guest. And call me Arnold."

The Purple Onion moved his saucer around. "Well, then let me thank all of you for this agreeable evening. Considering what just transpired out on the road, we might have spent this time differently."

"If I may, Mr. Onion, I disagree," said Brum.

"Storm," said the Purple Onion. "The Violet Storm."

"Of course," said Brum. "It's true if this were just another street fight, I'd run a sword through your neck right here. But since you invoked the sacred rite of the tourney, using the correct verbiage and all—thanks for looking that up, by the way, it really means a lot—we entered our martial contest under a flag of truce."

"Shucks, Lord Brum," said the Onion, rutabaga-mask wriggling on his face as he spoke, "that sure is chivalrous of you."

Brum rubbed the back of his head, slightly embarrassed.

"Well, chivalry is kind of what we do over at the Church of the Knight Errant. Our whole big thing."

"Nonetheless, breaking bread with you in this setting . . ." The Onion tore a brioche in half and put it down again. "This seems above and beyond."

"We have so few values," said Abhoc, smiling. "If we didn't at least adhere to our own tournament rules, we'd have nothing at all."

"We'd eat own flesh," said Heckley plainly.

"I would literally try to rape myself to death," said Abhoc.

For a long moment, the five others watched Abhoc try to feed tea cakes into his mouth around the high metal collar on his jaw.

"Mr. Onion, may I ask where did you get that skewer?" said Heckley. "I've seen a lot of jousting equipment in my day, and I can tell yours is optimally weighted and balanced. Without a doubt, Lord Brum would still have killed you, but you have a really nice skewer. Where did you get it?"

The Purple Onion dabbed his mask with the corner of a napkin. "Why thank you! My mechanic designed it for me. When he heard the Horsefolk were attacking, he said that I should have a lance, and he went down to the forge and made one for me."

"That's a skewer by the way," said Heckley. "Just like swords for fencing, jousting weapons are categorized by size and weight. Yours is a skewer. Lord Brum's here, that'd be, what'd you call . . ."

Heckley searched for the word.

"Ass-rammer!" A heavy fist smashed the table and made the china tinkle.

"An ass-rammer. Correct, Sir Abhoc." Heckley leaned on the table, his elbow in a saucer. "Anyways, what quick work for your mechanic. When did we announce our plans? Yesterday afternoon?"

The Onion glanced away to the right. "Not *so* quick. That is why I was late, he was dallying with the grip."

"Superb craftsmanship, though. I could see how effortless it was to wield and aim. Not only that: the design really coordinates with the rest of your accoutrement. You made a good visual impression out there. Lordly, but totally mod. Your man is quite an asset."

"Well, I pay him," the Onion said, crossing his arms uncomfortably.

Bubo tsked.

"Yes, but when someone goes above and beyond like that," said Heckley, "you need to take time to thank him. Say it and really mean it, don't just clear him a bonus."

"But also clear him a bonus," said Abhoc.

The four faces of the Pestilence leaned forward expectantly to hear how someone was getting a raise.

Arnold rolled his eyes at the Onion. *Poors, am I right?*

"Still," said the Onion awkwardly, "I find ourselves at an impasse. You gentlemen have been so hospitable, but I am sworn to protect Dodoville. Unfortunately, I cannot permit you to continue to lay waste to the city. I don't suppose you'd be willing to disappear back into the Kolkheks and never return?"

"Not a chance," said Brum, his mustaches shaking solemnly. "But I can offer you this. Our next target is Club Towers, down on the Siding. Why don't we meet there and resume our conflict in an honorable fashion?"

"I would very much like that," said the Onion, "but I'm afraid you have me at a disadvantage. My automobile has been badly compromised in this encounter. I'm not sure I could get there in time to be of service to any survivors."

Brum waved a hand. "We'll have to make some field repairs as well. My engine took some damage from that anti-horse ballista. A very fine shot, Arnold, by the way!"

"Thank you, Horace," said Arnold, "that's very kind of you."

Brum smashed a wall with his fist, sending splinters of onyx everywhere. "Address me in the familiar, will you?! I'll empty your impudent throat right here at the table!"

"Lord Brum, I meant no dis—"

Brum smiled. "Just kidding, Horace is fine. In any case, Mr. Onion—"

"Storm."

"We usually like to put on a show before we start the slaughter anyway—that's just our modus of operation—so that should give you ample time . . ."

"Very generous of you, my good sirs," said the Onion, rising from the table. "But I should probably get a head start, seeing my car is wedged inside the ancient grotto this lovely house is built upon."

"It's a very sacred site for the indigenous population," said Arnold with an air of pride, "I receive irate correspondence about it on a regular basis. You should come tour it sometime. What's left of it."

The Onion bowed slightly. "If I were not an anonymous vigilante, I would certainly take you up on your offer."

"Come in costume!"

"Oh, I couldn't. By the way, do you happen to have a winch motor I could hook my tow cables up to? It's really lodged in there good."

"My Manners! Absolutely." Arnold stood. "Sirs. My lord. Excuse me."

The Pestilence watched the two men leave the room. Abhoc stirred very loudly while the others sipped their tea. Moments passed in silence.

At last, Heckley spoke.

"What do you think, Lord Brum, should we kill him now?"

Brum and Bubo exchanged a look. Abhoc munched on whatever Trader Joe's bullshit Anne had laid out.

"We swore an oath," said Brum.

Abhoc spoke with his mouth full. "But do we really want that guy at our dance party? He's such a square!"

Bubo shrugged. "We could just ask the bouncer to not let him in."

Three pairs of eyes stared down the smaller knight.

"He's a stand-up guy," Bubo assured them. "The Purple Onion won't get past without his say-so!"

Abhoc made a rude gesture with one hand while cramming food in his face with the other.

"I'll decide when we finish our samosas," said Brum quietly.

On the wall, a little wooden bird emerged from its trap door. It cried cuckoo six times before the clock fractured into a dozen pieces.

"Thank you, Sir Abhoc," said the Knight Commander.

Heckley stared forlornly at his empty cup.

"I'll be mother," said Bubo, pouring everyone a refill from the teapot.

•

Arnold and Anne Fleck stood on the front lawn, watching the hedges burn themselves out. A strong wind off the mountain had spread the flame, and hardly a shrub in Prismton remained but the cinders.

"Twenty years," said Anne. "The twenty best years of my life given to you and this imbecile paradise. All I asked in return was the chance to kill one Horselord. *One* fucking anachronistic cocksucker on a zebra!"

"I know, Anne."

She smelled of burnt hair. He smelled of burnt rubber. Dislodging the Onion's car had taken effort.

"Not five fucking minutes," said Anne. "I get here just in time to watch you crash some fucking dick-mobile through my living room window! Holy shit, I think. There's my house. Getting fucked to death by a literal house-fucking dick car!"

Arnold rubbed his temples. "Yes, Anne, I saw."

"It does like ten goddamn donuts through the furniture before it comes to a stop. And now those fucking *horsefuckers* are sitting in my breakfast nook—"

"It's a vesper nook."

"There's no such *fucking thing* as a vesper nook! They're eating tea and hors d'oeuvres, for fuck's sake. Which I had to serve *myself* because *somebody* lanced the maid's forehead to a fucking tree!"

"Maybe it was suicide, Anne, did you think of that? God knows it's no more than I've dreamt of! I don't even . . ."

Arnold sighed. He didn't have the energy for this.

"Why did you invite them in?" he asked instead. "They came here to kill us and destroy our house!"

"Destroying our house was *your* idea, Arnie! They just came to kill each other!"

"Well, they didn't come for tea!"

"Ugh!" Ann tore at her hair in rage. "People talk. All these miserable back-terrace cunts *do* is talk. They can't wait for a chance to spread it everywhere what a shitty host I am."

"The town's on fire for Christ's sake!" Spittle flew from his lips in frustration.

"I know that. *They* know that. But do you think they care?

102

They don't give a fuck. Any chance they get. Any fucking chance!"

"No one's going to be talking about your spread tonight. Believe me."

"Honey mustard! Instead of peanut sauce, I put out *honey mustard* because the pantry had a *giant dick* in it and they're sorta both the same fucking color!"

Arnold took a deep calming breath. "Forget about it," he said quietly. "Everything is dick-colored these days, honey."

Anne screamed. "Honey *mustard!* Like it's nineteen ninety-fucking-three."

The thought of it overwhelmed her and she fell to her knees. Arnold held his wife as she sobbed herself out.

Together they watched the Bratmobile limp away with its smashed chassis. Later, the Pestilence came out and got back on their horses. Everyone thanked the Flecks profusely for their hospitality, and Anne smiled and spoke cheerfully as if it were just another day.

When the last turbo thruster had disappeared over the hill, Anne pulled off her shapeless red dress and threw it atop the smoldering hedge fire. She marched back into the house in her slip, without a word to Arnold as she passed.

Arnold sat on the grass and buried his head in his hands. The Prism had been shattered. His home was ruined. His marriage was in shambles. All the dirt from his past was about to come to light. And his daughter . . . Would Morgana ever speak to him again?

Worst of all, the horses had escaped. If only he'd killed one goddamn steed . . .

The acrid scent of pipe tobacco filled his nostrils. His neighbor, Hals Crick, was standing over him.

When he looked up, a glass of cognac was placed in his hand. Crick took a seat on the grass beside him.

"Is the fire department dead too, or . . ."

Hals nodded. "Heads impaled on pikes in the plaza. Above the dog spa, all in a row."

Arnold sniffed his snifter. At least this was the good stuff. "How does it look?" he asked. "The impalement."

"Oh, impeccable. Say what you will, but Horsefolk really do good work."

How many times had the two men watched dark smoke curl from this very spot? In fact, their friendship was built on watching the infamous Dodoville arson fires in the mid-1990s. But never before had the conflagration been so close to home. Or anywhere near it really.

"So you built an anti-horse ballista in your garage," Hals said at last.

Arnold said nothing, stinking of stale sweat. At this point, acknowledgment seemed as ridiculous as denial.

"My neighbor and friend of twenty years," said Hals quietly, "there are things you have not told this community about yourself."

One hand. If only he had drenched one hand in stallion's blood, he would have left a gory print over Hals' face and walked off. But he stood there defeated, humiliated. A man who had gambled everything for far too little and lost.

"I've checked the municipal records," said Hals. "I know you are not who you say you are."

Arnold watched the crows flock over the town plaza. The corpses of servants had been piled there, he'd heard.

"No," he said.

"Who created this identity for you? Whose not quite perfect inspiration is Arnold Fleck?"

Arnold had retired from the gang life decades ago, but it still raised his hackles to think of ratting out someone who had done him a favor. To be honest, he didn't know if the counterfeiter was alive or dead. He'd never even met the man. Still, he would gain nothing by betraying him now.

"It's been so many years," he said. "I no longer remember the name."

"Think harder, Fleck. Or should I say, Vincent La Ropa?"

Arnold was silent.

"Was it by any chance Melvar Ferrato?"

"I don't know that name."

"Oh you don't?" cried Hals. "Interesting. Everyone in Dodoville who ever wanted to leave their old life behind knows that name. Except you."

Arnold said nothing.

"Let me show you something, Fleck."

Hals unbuttoned his shirt. Below the left nipple was a prison tattoo of a ferret. He held the shirt open just long enough for Arnold to identify the creature before buttoning back up.

"We're all criminals in Prismton. All former gang workers who rose as others fell. Surely you've noticed that none of the ways to make a fortune in Dodoville are legal. Or did you really believe we were the exceptions, the ones with clean hands? You've always been one of us, Fleck. It's only yourself you've been hiding from."

For a long moment, Arnold remained silent. Nothing Hals said had come as a surprise, but for some reason, he'd never put it all together.

"Everything's gone now," Arnold lamented. "The ancient community beyond the reach of gang violence. It's finally reached this place. We've been razed to the ground."

"Nonsense," said Hals Crick. "What we lost today was only possessions. The things we bought with money. The community remains. We're, what do you call . . ."

"A family?"

"No, not Casa Nostra. More like a syndicate. And it exists for one purpose: to guarantee that just as down there it is impossible to succeed, up here it is impossible to fail. Do you think you are the first of us to do something brain-dead stupid? You destroyed your ancient house. Fine. As a community, we'll build you a new ancient house. Together we'll get it done."

"But I can't ask—"

Hals shook his head. "You'd do the same for us. You'd have

106

no choice, actually, it's in the town charter. Otherwise, your whole family would be tortured to death." Hals smiled. "Trust me, Fleck, everything will be all right."

This really was a comfort to hear.

"Hals, I think they killed your son."

"What?"

"Yeah, he was wearing a Red Guard uniform. Like for Chairman Mao? To be ironic, you know. And—"

"Ah." Hals sighed and nodded. "The wife and I bought him at a flea market in Rio. Midge could never give birth to her own children. A baby would shatter those brittle hips into a thousand pieces."

Arnold waited for his neighbor's face to give something away.

"His grave will make a lovely lawn ornament," said Hals. "I'll say it's the tomb of my ancestor."

"But. Everyone knew Corey."

"And now everyone will say he was my great-great-grandfather. That's the kind of people we are. I'm sorry you've never appreciated the strength of the community that has embraced you. But we will be here for you, through times fair and foul."

Arnold returned Hals' smile and offered his hand.

"So long as you never touch me," Hals said. He stared at the hand like a dead possum until it went away.

"Right." Both men grinned.

"Listen, Fleck, here's what you're going to do. First, you are going to go back inside and tell any surviving servants they are fired—but feel free to reapply for their position once the new house is completed. Then you are going to take a fistful of whatever's in your medicine cabinet and get a good night's sleep. When you wake up, a construction crew will already be at work building you a new home no better than anyone else's."

"Thanks, Crick, I appreciate it."

"Then you'll find your wife, probably curled up in a half inch of water flooding the basement. You'll get some blankets and assure Anne everyone's talking about how well she represented our community to the Purple Onion and those men from the Church of the Knight Errant. You will find a way to be convincing."

Arnold nodded. "Okay, I'll do that."

"Good."

Hals took a puff from his pipe and blew several perfect smoke rings. He watched them dissipate as the first stars appeared in the night sky.

"Seriously, though," he said. "Honey mustard?"

"I know. What a bitch."

•

"How can I be of service, Master Victor?"

The skiapod appeared as a hologram on the comm display of the Purple Onion's motorcycle as it jetted down the

International Kolkhek Highway at 250 kph, en route to break the power of the Horsefolk once and for all.

"Mori, that Pestilence just scolded me," the Onion said in his digital voice.

"Well, they have worked very hard to be a plague upon this city. You're giving them a bad day. You can't expect politeness in return."

Victor switched off his voice filter.

"But they *were* polite, that's what irritates me. They said . . ." He paused.

The hologram bowed slightly at the waist. "Tell me anything, sir."

"They said I don't respect you enough, Mori. For the work you do. They don't think I'd be worth a damn without you."

Silence.

"And what is your feeling about that?"

"Well, I'm peerless in hand-to-hand fighting. I speak eleven languages and have top-tier computer programming skills. I've implemented the most comprehensive surveillance system any city has ever seen. But . . ."

"What is it, sir?"

"I'm not good at science."

Mori's digital outline shrunk in pain. "Oh, don't say that, Master Victor!"

"No, it's true. I know my aptitude for it is uncanny. Like, move over Max Planck."

"Absolutely, sir."

"But ever since Mother died while I was working on the high school science fair . . ."

"Oh, I know, sir!"

"I just couldn't science fast enough to save her *and* get the blue ribbon."

"But you tried!" The skiapod bobbed encouragingly, his eyes enormous and bright. "Curing a genetically-engineered master-virus is a lot to ask of a seventeen-year-old. And please consider: after all these years, there's still no treatment for it today."

"Because I stopped doing the work! Anyways, that's my Achilles heel. I have to rely on you to do science for me, even though you are the housekeeper and an endangered species."

"Oh, Master Victor, think of me as an asset, not a liability." Mori laid both hands over his heart. "Since the time of Alexander the Great, my people have been hunted across the globe with extreme prejudice. Murder parties of thousands would venture into a haunted jungle just to track down and slaughter a handful of us. Today, I don't even know if any others of my kind are left."

"I could put a research team on it."

"I've done my best not to find out, so I can't betray them under torture."

"Oh, I see. Well, as regarding my problem then."

"What I'm saying is, thirty-five years ago, your father and saintly mother took me in and entrusted me with the great responsibility of doing every last little thing in their vast household."

"That was pretty nice of them."

"Yes, it was. I served them over the course of three gang wars, while everyone else was under suspicion of treachery. Think of their faith in me! Instead of being ostracized and humiliated, I was allowed to feel I had value."

"Father is still kind of a prick, though."

Mori's childlike smile appeared. "Your family—you, Master Victor—have permitted me a purpose in a world that rejects me."

"So, you are saying you do what you do out of gratitude?"

Mori giggled playfully. "Not at all. What I mean is, the moment my ties are severed with the Cumins, I'll either be executed as a monster or cut up as a science experiment."

"Experiments? Oh, dear Mori, what would anyone ever want to know about you?"

"As a skiapod, my genetics provide me with only one leg. Which means I don't have a crotch. Haven't you ever wondered where I keep my genitals?"

"Just blown. Mind totally blown."

"My point, sir, is you don't have to respect me for what I do for you."

"I just assumed you were just asexual, like a smurf or Santa Claus."

"Because if the Purple Onion is ever killed in pursuit of his rather dubiously-defined vendetta—"

"God damn it, Mori! I'm the Violet Storm!"

". . . my options are either a painful death or decades of public degradation as some kind of circus freak. So I literally have no choice but complete dedication to you and the success of whatever off-kilter plans you hatch."

"Geez, Mori. Knowing that really does put my mind at ease."

"You are very welcome, Master Victor!"

The Purple Onion fired a finger pistol at Mori's hologram. "I know that now!"

The two laughed heartily.

EPISODE FIVE:

THE KEENING AT CLUB TOWERS

THE PESTILENCE turbo-boosted back into Dodoville. Emergency repairs to Brum's engine had made his mount battle ready again but not highway reliable, so Heckley, Abhoc, and Bubo towed the giant mare on a flatbed while Brum sat like Napoleon in the saddle. The trailer was decorated with flowers and a banner that read LONG LIVE THE HORSELORDS. The lettering was freehand, and the reverse side promised 10% off any carton of cigarettes with a purchase of a cinnamon broom. The floral arrangement featured rustic wildflowers with muted golds, dark greens, creams, and cerulean blues, all quite tastefully set out.

The Peers of the realm arrived in the Siding, a municipal district nestled inside a meander of the River Dodos. During the mid-twentieth century, it had been home to the local aluminum industry, whose gangland bosses ruled Dodoville with an iron fist—so to speak. Around the time of the Zahzian War, the impresario of the Mountebank Theater, himself a brutal crime lord, drove the metal workers out of the Siding and used the thick-walled buildings to defend his own interests in the city, including venues for the most lavish entertainments in Sporqia.

Today, Club Towers was the last remnant of either empire. (And it was only one building: that thing across the street was a parking garage.) Ostensibly built as a storage silo, it had stood sentinel in the gang wars over a choke point along the river. Now it simply housed nine dance clubs stacked one atop the other.

Its most conspicuous feature was a ramp that wound around the outside of the building like a barber's pole. At the start of the evening, you rode a crystal elevator to the top and worked your way down, or if you tended to gain energy as the night progressed, you started at the bottom and partied your way up. Halfway along your journey, you'd meet your soulmate and fall in love. Soon you'd learn you were traveling in opposite directions and never see each other again. At any point in this divine comedy, you could vomit off over the side of the ramp into the moat below.

"Admit four, please," said Abhoc at the gate. Here in the club lighting, the metal cone on his neck looked like a popped polo collar.

"Appropriate attire only," said the bouncer.

"We're wearing nothing but leather pants and riding boots," said Abhoc. "This is exactly appropriate."

The bouncer pointed behind them. "I'm talking about your companions. No one is allowed in here wearing a bit and bridle. Otherwise, we get perverts."

"This is a war hammer," Heckley explained, raising his weapon.

"And that meets dress code. But the practice of bondage is illegal in Dodoville where alcohol is sold. I don't make the rules, I enforce them."

The riders glanced at each other. Brum nodded.

"I think we'll just admit ourselves," said Abhoc.

The bouncer sighed. "Suit yourself." He pushed a button on his wristband. The steel portcullis behind him slammed shut, and a two hundred pound bar of solid oak slid into place to shore up the inside. "Now are you gonna go quiet, or do I have to call upstairs for them to start boiling the oil?"

The Pestilence huddled.

"Suggestions?" asked Brum.

"Seige Warfare 101," said Abhoc. "We hew down that statue over there with our laser-axes, then we can load it on the flatbed and use it as a battering ram."

"Too many steps," said Heckley. "Let's just harpoon that oak bar with our rope guns, then pull out the gate with our turbo thrusters."

"That moat is like three-quarters puke," Abhoc observed. "Why don't we fill it into balloons and lob them over the walls? Eventually, the smell will make them open up from the inside."

"These are all great ideas," said Bubo softly, "but I have a better way. Ker-poo-to-tweet!"

•

Mandi Dugin got off the trolley outside Club Towers, the Babylonian edifice that rose like a vulgar gesture toward heaven. At the base, the moat churned with discarded cocktails, broken glass, torn clothes, heelless pumps, even an ear or two. Here in Dodoville, this is where you came to dance, to drift through the scent of cologne tinged with fresh perspiration, to reunite with friends and forget yourself in the close press of strangers.

It had been a year since Mandi had gone out on the town. A year since the Archivists made their unexpected stop at her apartment. She and her boyfriend, Sven, had been making dinner when she ran out to the grocery for some garlic. On her return, the shopkeeper downstairs said he'd seen the strange men in monks' robes making the climb up to her floor.

"I dunno if they took anything," he'd said. "I know better than to let them see me twice."

Her first thought: they had requisitioned her grandmother's antique rice cooker. It looked like an enormous alien saucership that might spin up into the sky at any moment and communicate across galaxies with flashing neon. Mandi might not have missed the cooker—for good reason no one built them like that anymore—except it was all she had left of the plucky old woman who had raised her after her parents were killed in the gang wars.

116

During Botanicist Era of the '90s, the bloom of Dodoville's culture attracted the attention of international collectors, for whom the relics of its long, eclectic history made excellent conversation pieces. When the Consortium of Tchotchke Merchants was formed, it promised to sell the city's innumerable material oddities abroad to help fund exciting new municipal projects. But to do that, it had to catalog whatever treasures citizens had stashed away. It had to build an Archive. So if you were Dodovillean, you lent the Consortium access to your junk. To your history and your memories. To your privacy. To your entire sense of self.

In exchange, you might get a sports stadium.

Whoooo, go Pharaohs!

With relief, Mandi saw the cooker still bubbling away on the stove.

Then she found the receipt on the kitchen counter.

1 Nordic, 1.8m, 12.9 st, make of Brundtland era (II), v. good condition.

The monospaced font of a portable typewriter. The blotchy blue ink of carbon duplicate. Stamped with the seal of the Archive's department of acquisitions.

1 Nordic. Sven.

She staggered over to a kitchen stool.

V. good in the trading card sense, i.e. not good, i.e. creases, discoloration, and some wear.

To which she thought "Fuck you, the Archive," but also "Goddamn it, some crunches wouldn't have killed you."

But also: "How can Sven be a Dodovillean relic? He wasn't even Dodovillean."

Despite having slumped down upon the stool, she found herself strewn across the floor. Her body was emitting an awful braying sound she hadn't been aware the human organism could make. She listened to it for a while.

And also: "Well, of course, a ganglord comes into your house and steals your property—what else is government for?—but not your people. Sven was people!"

Then also: "The past tense. Why am I using the past tense?"

The obnoxious noise, originating from somewhere between her ears, did not abate. If anything, it was getting louder.

Sven had left Trondheim in disgrace after getting caught corrupting the results of an important study on *Picea abeis,* the Norway spruce. Ever since the gangland regime of U Dodo's Department of Botany was toppled, Dodoville had become the one place on earth where nobody batted an eye at someone being both a botanist and a retired criminal. In this city, any gang operative who managed to stay alive till the dust settled had earned the right to rebuild their lives in peace.

Rebuilding is what he and Mandi had done. Something very close to a life together.

But why did the Consortium take him? What buyer would want a researcher who produced bad data? It didn't make any sense.

For many months after the disappearance, Mandi could barely force herself to go outside, for fear the Archive might requisition something else while she was gone. (Although what was left to lose?)

But then the Purple Onion had begun his war on the Consortium and its Archive. On YouTube, she had seen the battered faces in dun-colored robes dripping hot tears on the doorsteps of the homes they had violated.

Once upon a time, you could not touch an Archivist on pain of death. Now someone *was* touching them. With a fist!

As the Archivists became less bold, ordinary people like Mandi were finding the nerve to look them in the eye.

What more defiant gesture to make against the Archive than to express joy again in public? To wear her slinkiest dress and dance in the company of others? Soon evil would be afraid to show its face in the light.

Did Mandi believe that? No. But it would be a pleasure to behave as if that day was coming.

For her, joy was an act of courage. Tonight she was taking back her life.

•

The Storm Cycle turned onto the streets of the Siding, the engine hammering like a hot summer rain on a corrugated metal roof. Over his spider silk bodysuit, Victor Cumin had donned purple riding leather with mint green and atomic tangerine trim. Running lights crisscrossed the chassis of his bike like a network of veins, and their hazy glow wrapped it in a luminous cloud that seemed to carry him over the asphalt.

As he passed, a raver whispered to his date: "Look, hon, it's the Onion Chopper!"

As Victor pulled up to Club Towers, he could see the Pestilence was already inside: the flash of the turbo thrusters appeared like the light of the will o' wisp as it circled one of the upper floors where shrieks and screams emanated.

Someone was probably serving free jello shots.

"ID please," said the bouncer at the door.

"I'm the Violet Storm," said the Purple Onion.

"I need some ID."

The Onion unzipped his motorcycle jacket to show the insignia on his chest.

"That is not a valid form of identification." The beefy doorman stared off at nothing, chewing on a toothpick.

"You let the Pestilence in."

"Who's he."

"Four men dressed like Vikings mounted on hooved quadrupeds. You can't have missed them."

The bouncer crossed his arms adversarially. "Which four?" he asked.

"They were the only ones." Victor's digital voice shook with extra reverb. "Don't tell me I don't know a thing I know!"

"They had ID."

"They are a horde of anti-government guerrillas on jetpack horses. You're saying they revealed their identities to you?"

The bouncer shrugged. "They said they're not afraid anymore."

Horace Brumfield. Martial Heckford. Bob Schyman. Only Abhoc used a true pseudonym. Even still . . .

"You sure they weren't fakes?"

"I've been a bouncer a long time. I know all the tricks."

Victor pulled something out of his chopper's top box. "Here's my ID."

The bouncer squinted at him and shined a flashlight down at the card. He studied it forever.

"This is the photo of a man who's had plastic surgery to look like you, Mister . . . Vargas."

"That is literally insane," said Victor.

"Don't tell me I don't know a thing I know."

No lie. The bouncer knew all the tricks.

Victor surveyed the tower. Even if he took out the bouncer, he'd never get past the portcullis: that thing had withstood battering rams during the Aluminum Age. He could rope gun up to one of the ramps, but then he'd have to face turbo horses without the Storm Cycle. Plus, he really didn't want to sneak in. In fights like this, it almost doesn't matter what happens, all anyone will remember tomorrow is your entrance.

What was the coolest entrance anyone ever made on a motorcycle?

He looked up into the sky.

Hagrid. The answer is Hagrid, right?

"Mori?"

"Yes, sir." A staticky voice on his wrist comm.

"Fire up the Storm Fighter. I'm going to need your help."

•

The Pestilence ascended the ramp around Club Towers at a walk, horses in a synchronized four-beat gait, heavy heads bobbing in half time inside their terrifying skull masks. The party-goers slunk aside to let them pass, their boisterous conversation falling silent in awe of the demons that had appeared unsummoned in their midst.

For almost a century, horses had been banned within Dodoville. Over that time, stories were told and retold how in the ancient past, the horse had been an instrument of fright and terror. It had borne fire and sword to burn houses, slaughter children and livestock, steal wealth, and trample the holy images. Tonight, these towering and robust specimens of mythical monsters had leaped from the tousled dreams of the tipsy revelers. Skintight silk armor wrapped the powerful limbs, and the musculature rippled beneath.

The knights rode high in the saddle, reins slack and faces straight ahead, so their dark countenance would not discourage curious on-lookers from their fill of the spectacle. A reckless few even stretched out a hand to feel the hot air snorted from the nostrils, to touch the coarse hair of the tail before it flicked away in annoyance.

"Okay," whispered Abhoc into his headset, "I understand beating up the cops. I understand smoking out those rich pricks in the suburbs. I guess people on the train make sense too, on account they ain't making the commute on horseback as is gentlemanly. But why are we terrorizing people out just having a good time?"

"Just a good time?" spake Lord Brum. "Any joy that giveth not strength to resurgent Camelot striketh a blow 'cross the equine jaw of the 'Folk. For anyone who releaseth an endorphin into him'es system without rage in him'es heart, whosoever take-parteth in youth culture not in service to an uberlord but frolicke him a-mit theym who singen without frivol and squander him'es movement onto no profit: why, these be our most dangerful foe-ems."

"I agree, m'Lord," said Heckley. "Sack, sword, and saddle! But also, how so?"

"Do you think the Lord Harthur had time to enjoy himself when the evil wizard Symerlus stole the Sacred Grobbet from him'es table? Or when he challenged Sir Pontius to the joust at Gethsema Crossing? Or when Galahad fell ill with trolleprosy, and Lord Harthur reached out his holy hand to restore him'es virginity, bidding him whore no more?"

"Not during these times, Knight Commander," said Abhoc, "but maybe after. Or before?"

Brum reined his horse so fierce, it whinnied as it came round. He glowered back at his men, the lines in his forehead reading like a prophecy of doom.

"Then for the mighty deeds God hath fulfilled through ye by sun's witness, pay back to heaven with merriment 'neath sign of the moon. Enjoy yourselves! That's an order." Here Brum smiled. "And by Christ's spurs, hurt no one!"

"By bright Signo," swore Heckley.

"By the sweet sands of Camelot," cried Abhoc.

"We swear it shall be so!" pledged Bubo.

Abhoc leaned over and punched the nearest person so hard, you could hear the sternum crack as the body fell limp into the arms of the crowd.

"Oops," he said. "Hand slipped."

"S'all right," said Brum evenly. "None can promise more than can be done."

•

Sometimes when the cinder cone of Mt. Myrtle fulminated at dusk, the sky god's thunder stirred the seething cauldron of earth till tendrils of smoke billowed up and stained the dome of heaven with a purplish tinge—magenta, as if sky's azure had mixed with the deep red of the lava fissures.

The Storm Fighter was a sleek aircraft lit nose-to-tail in the selfsame hue. Like a seed spit from the teeth of the volcano, it tore through the sky, the scream of its engines an echo of the dyspeptic earth, its contrails like the steam that rose from the craggy vents in the rock.

Mori had constructed it out of salvage from MiGs and other heavy machinery the Soviets had left behind after the Zahzian War.

Sitting the cockpit now, the flight helmet ill-fitting upon his bulbous head, he glanced down at the city. Undoubtedly, people who had heard the aircraft cutting the lower atmosphere were now pointing up at the plane's gaudy lights.

In Dodoville, they called it the Onion Wing.

Towing clamps secured the Storm Cycle to the underside of the plane. In the bike's saddle, Victor Cumin awaited deployment, to be flung into battle as his vigilante alter ego. Over the comm, Mori heard him humming to himself, which meant he was chomping at the bit to launch.

A skiapod's lifespan naturally outlasts countless generations of men. Across the centuries, Victor Cumin was hardly the first thrill-seeking lunatic Mori had been tasked with keeping alive. But he was certainly among the most challenging.

Sitting in the Storm Fighter's cockpit made Mori's stomach flip. Heights didn't bother him—once a month he'd climb out onto the roof of the solarium to wash the glass panels—but no matter how well he understood flight mechanics, the modern practice of taking to the sky still felt like sorcery.

"Master Victor, couldn't you find another way into Club Towers? I say this because trajectory mathematics is extremely difficult."

Mori glanced nervously at the handwritten equations scotch-taped to the instrument panel.

"I don't want to hear you don't know how to do this, Mori." The wind-battered voice from under the plane came in choppy over the comm.

"Sir, I changed your diapers when you were a babe. I've long known it was only a matter of time before you asked me to toss you from an airplane on a motorcycle. I just assumed when that day came, I'd have more than half an hour to prepare the drop coordinates."

"The Pestilence is already inside. Who knows what damage they've done!"

That wasn't a flight of geese he heard on Victor's comm. It couldn't be. Certainly not.

"Yes, but. I heard a fifteen-year-old girl once got in with a letter from her phys. ed. teacher."

"Listen, Mori. You're not human, so this may not make sense to you: The Pestilence has laser shields, flamethrowers, turbo saddles, not to mention a totally bitchin' onboard sound system. If I am going to show the people of Dodoville that the Violet Storm is on the side of right, I have to have waaaay more awesome gear. Do you understand?"

"Let's pretend I do."

"The way to do that is to make the better entrance. Fortunately, the Pestilence just used the front door, so I'm going to jump my custom-made chopper out of my custom-made jet, and it land it on the roof without a parachute."

"Wait, what?"

"I'm using the repulsion thrusters. It's too dark to see a parachute, but the thruster glow is neon purple. That's called branding."

"You . . . Master Victor, you'll be killed for sure."

"You said with these thrusters I could drive this bike off any building in town."

"Yes, but." Mori dipped the plane and got out a calculator. "The *Spyhole* Building is only eleven stories tall. To bring you in at a safe altitude, I'm really going to have to buzz these rooftops."

"The better to hear the engines by. I don't want anyone to miss the show for lack of hoopla."

"Club Towers is in a canyon. I hope I'll have time to pull out."

"I've done it a dozen times. Easy peasy."

"For you, Master Victor. I don't have much flight experience. Remember, I belong to a species that chose extinction over action sequences."

"Just keep your head, Mori. You'll be fine."

If fine meant shaking and nausea, then Mori was indeed fine.

"Apropos of nothing, sir, may I remind you the only job I'm contracted to perform for you is washing the linen."

"You have a contract? I thought you just didn't dare to leave, on account of being a freak and all. No offense."

"I signed with your father forty years ago, after he rescued me from that hunting party on the Savanna."

"I thought my father *was* the hunting party."

"I don't recall, sir," said Mori quietly.

"How can you not recall? He chased you across three continents."

Mori sighed. "The safety clamps have disengaged. You will

launch automatically when we reach the drop point. I hope my calculations are correct, I had to relearn the mathematics on the flight over."

"Say again?"

"Godspeed, sir."

On the monitor, Mori watched the chopper detach from the jet's underbelly. Victor's backside immediately flew out of the seat. He hung on only by the handlebars as the bike dead dropped through the sky.

"No time for tricks, sir! You need to activate that thruster!"

"Help! The bike's chassis is too aerodynamic, it's slicing through the air like a hot knife. All I can manage is to hold on."

Muttering something in the extinct skiapod language, Mori rolled the plane and pushed the stick forward hard in a split S maneuver. As the inside loop crushed him against his seat, he closed his eyes and paid honor to every dead relative he could name going back four generations.

The leveling plane flew so low, it sucked dish antennae off the taller buildings.

"Weapons engaged," said the computer. "Targeting systems online."

"Shut yourself off, targeting systems," said Mori. "You're not programmed for this kind of insanity."

Static on the comm.

"Repeat that, Mori. I didn't copy."

"I said you're in good hands, sir. Everything under control." He disengaged the launch safety and set aim for empty space. "I can't believe I'm doing this," he muttered.

A missile sizzled off the starboard wing.

"Brace yourself, sir, this may sting a bit."

A scream stymied Victor's response as the projectile exploded between the motorcycle and the ground, blasting the bike seat hard against his posterior.

"That's great, Mori, you just blew me off target."

"Hold tight, sir."

The Storm Cycle showed as little more than a shadow against the city lights below.

"Two pi r raised to the angular dispensation ratio times the mass-to-energy coefficient . . ."

"Mori, are you casting a spell?"

"I hope so, sir." He banked hard to the left. The airspeed gained from his previous maneuver created a huge vacuum, which as the Storm Fighter blasted by, pulled the chopper back into its wake.

Enough. But maybe too much?

The bike continued to free fall.

"Thrusters!" Mori screamed. "Damn it, sir, what are you doing?"

The Chopper came to life with a pair of vibrant neon purple glows. They were spinning one over the other. The flyby had sucked the bike into a lateral roll.

"Stabilizers!" Mori cried.

"I'm looking! Where the hell are they?"

"Jesus, right next to the—"

"Got it."

The spinning began to slow. The motorcycle came at the concrete tower at a sharp angle, and Victor's head, inverse on the bike, barely cleared the retaining wall as he passed over. The Storm Cycle's wheels hit the roof with a thump. The front tire stood pivot while the rear of the bike flared out behind him.

Victor barely had a moment to orient himself when someone smacked him on the helmet, thrust a drink in his hand, and began flashing selfies in his face.

"Whoooo! An Onion's here to spice this party *up!*"

Victor leaped from his bike and staggered to the edge of the roof. Pulling off both his bike helmet and the face mask beneath it, he vomited over the retaining wall.

The crowd roared in approval. The rooftop DJ turned up the volume. Someone got Victor another drink.

"Chopper to Storm Fighter," he said, reapplying his mask. "Storm Fighter, this is Chopper. I am in the club. Repeat. I am in the club."

"Roger that, Chopper," said Mori wearily.

Time to head home and beat out the living room rugs.

The Storm Fighter rose sharply out of the canyon, splitting the night with an aerial scream the citizens of Dodoville had not heard since the Zahzian air raids of the early 1980s. Everyone in town over forty beshit their pants with such violence, the mass-soiling would be discussed with nostalgia for weeks to come.

Mandi worked her way through the crowd, meeting glances, dancing until the attention waned, then slipping away. Music thrummed in her body as she and a stranger performed sensual co-auditions with their hands and hips, a pantomime of *what I need, what I offer, who I'm pretending to be*. Couples pressed together around her, groups of three or five, bodies jerking to the rhythm, clothes exposing the flesh most vulnerable to animal predation, an almost sleepy look in their eye. Everything about them conveyed indifference to danger. Welcome to Night on Earth.

What they're really doing, she thought, *is crying out for protection.*

In this place, the noise would swallow any cry of distress.

She was not afraid to bare her vulnerability. *In Dodoville, we've all been damaged,* she thought, *we all have hurts that don't heal. Sometimes they leave a scar others find alluring. Sometimes they stamp you for the discard pile.* She worried the marks beneath her flesh had deformed her, making her untouchable, and anyone could see them. They were visible in how she dressed and the way she moved. Inscribed across her face.

She'd never know why her best friend and lover had been killed. There was no one to ask, nowhere to investigate.

The day after they took Sven, she'd had no choice but to go to work. At the florist shop, even the cactuses looked like a funeral bouquet. Sometimes she would ask a customer to excuse her, then retreat to the backroom to scream and sob. She emptied herself efficiently, loudly and with force, then returned to work with a brave face. Meaning, she arranged flowers while she wept in a way that defied anyone to ask. Sometimes as she trimmed a steam, she cried out as if cutting off a piece of herself. Any show of concern she answered with a reviling look.

Mandi did this until close, then she went home.

She came in the next morning and did it again. She did this every day until it became who she was, someone who screamed and wept without provocation but who never seemed to notice. Whose demeanor bullied you into not noticing either.

In Club Towers, she realized she was screaming right now. Likely, she had been screaming all night. Anyone might think she was singing along. A little tone deaf, maybe.

The Purple Onion could force you to cry in front of everybody. Some said by reciting an incantation, others by splashing your face with a magic potion. Anyways, there was nothing you could do about it.

Last week, this guy had gotten caught stealing some valuable operation manuals for kitchen appliances, and the Onion made him tear his shirt and weep about boners or something. Everyone saw he had pretty much the weirdest body hair, like overused brush bristles. It was soooo gross, but she heard he was charging people to see it now.

The point was, if the Onion got you, no one could accuse you of being selfish and making a spectacle of yourself, 'cause you couldn't help it. The Onion was the spectacle-maker. You were just in the wrong place. It could happen to anyone.

•

"Hey, Sergeant Onion."

Victor turned. "Me?" He spoke the word into his noise-canceling face mask, whose software converted his speech into a soothing, untraceable computer-generated voice.

"Sorry Sarge, I hate to . . . I heard you radioing back to base. We're just *tailgating* the Club here. This is the parking garage across the street."

Now that the world was no longer spinning, Victor saw this was true. Kitty-corner across the intersection of Staple St. And Poptop Blvd., he made out the lights of the Pestilence's turbo thrusters and the glinting tips of their lances flitting around the nightclub two floors below. The screams of party-goers rose up to his ears. At the rooftop bar, a few dozen people were shouting toward where they'd seen a bolt of purple lightning strike the garage tower. They threw cocktail glasses in his general direction.

All in all, though, far less chaotic than you'd think a massacre would be.

"My name is Storm," said Victor, "and I'm not in the army, mister."

"Of course not, captain. I didn't mean to imply . . ."

"All right, private," Victor said sharply. "Gather up the men. Tell the DJ over there to break down his equipment and await my instructions."

He unloaded the Chopper's top box. As he assembled his electro-goad quarterstaff, he started making field modifications.

Someone was standing behind him.

Victor looked over his shoulder. The man wore a stovepipe hat encrusted with rhinestones, oversized sunglasses, skintight digicamo over his beefy chest, and a short pink scarf knotted like a tie around his neck.

"You the DJ?" Victor asked.

The man's fingers, fit inside cut-off leather gloves, folded around his biceps. "What are we building?" He sounded irritated.

"You're building a ramp. I'm reinforcing this thing to unhorse a knight of the realm. The sirs from the Church of the Knight Errant don't know yet but . . . they and I are having a tournament."

Victor attached a laser finial to the head of his staff and walked over to the edge of the roof. Brandishing its staticky light above his head, he signaled to the crowd atop the far tower to stay tuned.

Across the way, the revelers cheered. Perhaps because he had a glowing stick.

The DJ cleared his throat. "You want me to me arrange a mint's worth of my own sensitive equipment—the stuff I use to make my living—into a ramp for you to drive your motorcycle over. Did I hear right?"

"That is correct," said Victor. "I'm going to need a smooth acceleration because it's quite a gap. Can you do that?"

The DJ wrinkled his nose as he glanced at the sprawling chasm between buildings.

"It's not a question of 'can I,'" he said.

Victor gripped the man's shoulder. "Excellent," he said.

The Onion's leather jacket crackled as he slid back into the seat of the chopper. "Excuse me while I go throw down the gauntlet. Tonight we sky joust."

•

Around and around the tower they climbed, like pilgrims spiraling the road to paradise. At the door of each club, a small crowd gathered, sleek blazers and tight-fitting dress shirts, booty shorts and mesh net cleavage, asking with silent eyes if this was the circle the riders had been assigned to inhabit. Six doors called out to the knights with throbbing music and bartenders dressed like slaves upon an imperial pleasure barge, six doors they passed without glance or comment. At the seventh door, they stopped. Beyond the corbel archway, shining with brightly-colored bricks from a 1980s arcade game, assembled the largest, most boisterous crowd so far. Here was the legendary Rock Lobster.

The knights bowed their heads to pass under the lintel. Snorting wetly, the steeds picked their way through the crowd, peeling booty off crotch and crotch off booty.

"Watch yourself, jackass!" cried one reveler, one sheet to the wind too many, not realizing what had shoved him aside.

The man turned around to see his mistake. Brum lifted him off the ground by his limply-popped polo.

"Jackass?" cried Brum. "Rosemarie traces her lineage to the court of Charlemagne!" He laid the man cold with the back of a fist.

Like the teeth of a rake, the horsemen cut through the crowd to where the DJ stood at his station.

"What up, sirs?" he said, twinkling bracelet charms braided into his hair.

Heckley put a war hammer through one of his turntables.

"Lords? I meant m'lords! Chill, all right?"

"Scram. Or the next thing I smash is your skull."

"No problem. Only I can ask that you not touch the . . . Hey man, whatever you want. Mi casa es—"

Abhoc grabbed the disc jockey with both hands and heaved him across the neck of his horse. The skinny body skipped like a stone twice across the top of the crowd before falling to the ground.

"Are you ready, Sir Bubo?" asked Brum.

"Straining at the bit all week, Knight Commander!" Bubo hopped down from his steed and started adjusting the equalizer and queuing tracks. The headphones fit snuggly over his Teutonic helm.

"Ladies and gentlemen," called Heckley into the microphone. "Introducing . . . DJ Bubo Skyyyymole!"

Water. What?
Water. Where?
At the bottom of the ocean!

Water. What?
Water. Where?
At the bottom of the ocean!

The crowd shrugged and resumed dancing.

The remaining Pestilence ignited their laser bucklers and rode their steeds around the outside of the room. People hurled empty glasses, which shattered upon the barriers of light. As the fragments fell, the floor lights ignited them into shards of fire.

A weird flirtation took place between the Pestilence and the crowd, each daring the other closer then driving them back.

The knights' weaponry intimidated no one; in fact, many revelers had to return to the nine-to-five grind of the gang wars in the morning. But when the Pestilence's engines propelled them in synchronized bursts, tripling their speed as they looped around the revelers, few could say for sure whether machine or animal had manufactured the blue flare from the tail ends.

What were these impossible creatures? The elongated head, the huge iris-less eyes, the way they shook the floor with their step. If one had breathed fire at that moment, nobody would have been surprised.

Without warning, Abhoc caught a man in a gray sports coat behind the ear with a mace. The crowd saw his silhouette on the wall as his limp body sailed like a kite toward the neon chandelier. The strobe lights seemed to freeze the gobbets of blood midair.

DJ Bubo Skymole caught the dying man's image on a closed-circuit camera and, punching stills through various digital filters, posted them to screens around the room. He interspliced a two-second clip of the body striking the ground, boomeranging it forward and reverse, then spun a picture centered on the broken head bleeding out. These images kaleidoscoped upon the walls in an 80s love bubble style, backed by the noodly whine of synthesizers.

So many times in movies, a gunshot rings out in a club and everyone who's having a good time screams and stampedes the door. *None of those movies took place in Dodoville*, Heckley observed.

One by one, women in evening dresses knelt around the broken head in a semicircle, like the halo of a martyr. They tossed their hair; their upper bodies contorted and shook.

In other times and places, dance simulates war or sex. Here, a death rattle.

Elbows rigid, fingers splayed. Shaka-ka-kaka-ka-ka!

At the base of a volcano, Dodoville stood always at the precipice of annihilation. The earth grumbled, the body flailed and floundered but you didn't go over the edge, the fear remained inside you like a thing waiting to be born. When you saw a broken body, split open and pouring out the essence of life, you leaned closer so your death-fear might escape with the fallen's breath and soul.

They did not dance but flung their bodies at the music. They battered it down like a door with a ram. *In.* The blows thunderous, the boom giant and hollow. *In.*

They pressed toward the center of the room. *In.* Toward the holy icon splayed on the floor.

Pray pray pray pray pray.

The quadrupeds galloped, the clustered four beat suspended in silence as all four limbs left the ground, bearing four riders and harbingers of the end. *In.* Missiles of horse flesh clung to their arcs around the maelstrom swirling down into the center of the room.

The vortex of death drew them all in.

•

Mandi stared down at the brained man in the gray jacket and corduroy Converse. With one brutal gesture, he had gone from the evening's participant to its decor. An ornament of death, she thought, the way most people keep their grandfather's skull on the mantelpiece.

Whoever he had been, nobody was interested now.

A year ago, some other gesture—she'd never know what— had transformed Sven from the horizon in her life to someone's material inconvenience. Had that blow been this quick, this indifferent?

Mandi did not scream, she did not cry. She danced. The heels of her palms pressed hard on her knees. She snaked her spine and tossed her hair.

The knights circled the room, Dark Age armaments jangling from their saddles, Teutonic helmets atop naked torsos streaked with war paint. Now the horses were the music, the rhythm. From walk to canter to trot, their pace quickened. As they circled, she felt a pull drawing her closer and closer to the shallow-breathing man whose essence was escaping. Over the sound system, the staccato crash of the drum machine crackled out the time: her three-inch heel struck the floor like flint on steel, trying to coax out a spark to catch on the pageantry of the bacchanalia around her, to spread to every level of this edifice of perverse illusion, devouring the whole tower circle by circle in famished conflagration.

She had a recurring dream—she was remembering it only now—of a plague of locusts descending on Dodoville, but instead of crops, they devoured buildings and roads and statues, until they had consumed all the city's eccentric history, its bizarre culture, its pernicious but sometimes charming impulses. Then the winged pests flew right at her, they crawled inside her skull and gorged themselves on everything she had ever done, or been, or suffered. Now her face was like any other, it spoke the words other faces spoke, and only when it lay broken open in ruin could you see it ever had the potential to be anything else.

Behold these dreams made flesh. Horseflesh.

Nightmares. Physical embodiments of psychic terrors.

It was impossible for the slender legs of those beats to carry the bulk of body and rider, while still moving like grace itself.

Was this the breed that turned you to stone? Or the kind whose eyes robbed you of sanity?

At first, the vibration seemed to come from the subwoofers. The revelers heard the roar of the approaching fighter jet before they understood it.

The explosion shook the building at its foundation.

As if this were a signal, Heckley's heavy leather boot kicked open the double doors to the outside and let the night in. A flash of purple rent the sky, a ball of rolling fire.

A young woman in a Cyndi Lauper riot of skirts, beads, hair, and headbands, watched in awe as the mulberry light struck the garage across the street. Like an ancient monarch who did not expect the prophets' words fulfilled in her lifetime, she gazed up with a thrill of joy tinged with fear. Gingerly she leaned on the threshold to the dance hall. Neon-orange fingerless gloves.

Brum lanced her through the temple at a charge. As it passed behind her eyes, the metal shaft extinguished their light and erupted above her far ear. Spurring his horse, Brum hoisted her childlike body above his head, her jaw agape in a mockery of a scream, and swiveled her around to the back where she slid off the end of the lance.

If before the crowd had been indifferent to the murder of one of their number, with the jet's war scream and the exploding missile, now they panicked and ran for the door. Some pushed others forward to shield them from the horses. The three circling knights beat these back like a sadistic revolving door. Brum smashed with his hammer; Abhoc sliced with his sword; Heckley simply garroted them and dragged them out of the way. Clamped between the fear of being trapped in here and fear of pushing their way out, the crowd began to tear itself apart.

Mandi continued to dance. She elbowed and reveled as others fought and died. Belinda Carlisle made heaven a place on earth. Bon Jovi gave love a bad name. Oh whoa whoa, what?

Once again, an engine. An ostentatious roar from the garage across the street, a single headlight shining in on them.

The horses stopped, the body press ceased. A hazy purple glow peered in on them, casting the silhouette of the vigilante's insignia against the far wall. A dark storm cloud.

Anyone might mistake it for an onion.

In the parking garage across the street, the vigilante hoisted his makeshift lance, a golden staff with sparks crackling from the finial. Thrusting upward to indicate the roof, he kicked his bike into gear and rode up the ramp.

DJ Skymole cut the music and put up the houselights as he and his companions readied themselves to accept the challenge.

"About goddamn time," said Abhoc. "Another minute of that fucking noise, I might have had to hurt somebody."

•

"It's solid construction. A perfect incline, optimal takeoff angle. If your bike doesn't make the jump, fault the rider, not the ramp."

The tailgate DJ pointed at the structure behind him, six meters long rising gradually to meet the top of the retaining wall.

Although made of diverse materials, everything from an ironing board to a magician's teleportation box, the joints were seamless, as if made by design.

"Everything looks satisfactory," said the Onion. "Thank you."

The DJ really expected him to be more impressed.

The vigilante was tinkering inside his chopper, splicing cables in a way that didn't seem entirely safe.

"From equipment I had on hand," the DJ added. "Plus stuff people happened to have in their cars. If I yanked the sewing machine and the sushi kit, the whole thing would collapse."

"I believe that." Smoke rose from a soldering iron. The Onion did not look up from his work.

"I even added purple running lights, so it would look cool. Because I get it, you know. The need for aesthetics."

"As I said, good job."

The DJ's frustration started coming through.

"I'm a retired army corps engineer. I moved Soviet tanks through the Chalian swamps during the Zahzian War. You were about to hurl yourself off a building on whatever the DJ could cobble together at the last moment. Do you know how many guys who do this job sprinkle donuts during the day?"

The Onion stopped his modifications and stood to face the man.

"Sir, you have my sincere gratitude. Now if you don't mind,

I need to coax enough thrust out of this engine, else I won't clear the gap. Do you realize how foolish that would make me look?"

"Foolish?" the DJ cried in exasperation. "Don't you even want to inspect the ramp I built?"

Across the street at Club Towers, fanfare announced the Pestilence, who were emerging onto the roof in full tournament dress. A throng of dancers advanced before them, laughing and crying out their noble names.

"I trust you," the Onion said.

"You *trust* me?" The DJ raised both palms, recoiling like he'd be spat on. "All right, man. Try not to die." He turned away in disgust.

The Onion spun the man back around by the shoulder. He was more slender but a full head taller than the DJ. It can only have been an illusion, all the glitz and sparkle of a Dodoville night, but as the DJ looked beyond the mask into the vigilante's eyes, two golden pinpricks seemed to shine from the depths of his pupils, as if he were not a man at all—either something higher or more infernal.

The Onion's voice was eerily calm.

"I flew in here on a motorcycle riding a missile detonation. Death and I have a bargain. Do you think you have the power to alter the terms?"

For a long moment, the DJ was silent.

"I've seen too much to believe in magic powers," the man said, removing the vigilante's hand from his shoulder. "In this city, even the gods are mortal. So respect the grave. It won't respect you." Once again, he walked away.

The Onion kick-started his chopper and rode it up the ramp to the top of the retaining wall. Across the gap, Brum, Heckley, and Adhoc faced him upon on their steeds. They stood in chevron formation, lances held upright. The gleaming tips scraped the sky as it passed overhead, incising the night like shooting stars.

Bubo was off to one side, flying the colors and playing The Chemical Brothers from his saddle speakers.

The crowd of revelers stood about in silent expectation. Death riders in their midst, block-rocking beats pooling in their limbs, ready to unleash some yet undecided action.

To whose banner would they rally?

The Onion hoisted his quarterstaff, the golden finial cascading sparks on either side of his head, illuminating him like an angel.

It was time to win them over with an astonishing display of arms. It was time to pick a fight.

•

Abhoc saw the Onion appear atop the far wall. Black jumpsuit with highlights of orange and yellow, the helmet in his hand a deep purple. The caption of the photo in tomorrow's *Spyhole* would read "Arrogant Prick, Moments from Death." *Well, get on it then*, he thought. Abhoc enjoyed a sky joust as much as anyone, but he was eager to get back to his regular evening of binge drinking and murder.

"I'm going to make the jump," called the Onion beneath the mask. Tranquil as a spaceship computer before it goes rogue and seizes functions. "Unless one of you gallants has the courage and skill to unhorse me."

Brum's voice ground like a stone mill.

"We have both the skills and the high ground." The snapping of the Pestilence's banner in the wind filled the silences. "We have the favor of His Divine Majesty Harthur of Christwall. We have proper equipment too. I don't recommend jousting with a lance not weighted for the task. Why don't you come down and show your ID at the door like everyone else?"

Abhoc shared a quick smile with Heckley. A government issued driver's license. Onion comma Purple.

From the quarterstaff's spearhead finial sputtered another cascade of sparks.

Like blond hair churned by a putrid south wind. Like an impressionist haystack ravaged with lust for its first cousin. A seriously extravagant display of light.

"Choose your champion," cried the Onion, "so the earth which ye have blighted with evil, that man may cleanse with the storm of his tears!"

That was his cue. Abhoc's charger stepped forward. Heckley's too. The space-age horseshoes struck the surface of the roof with a clang.

Abhoc gazed back at Bubo, who with the shell of his

headphones pressed to his ear was oblivious to the world. He threw a dirty rag at the beat-bobbing face. Bubo startled. Abhoc snarled, and Bubo also ordered his horse forward.

"Let it be me, Lord Brum," said Heckley, stately as a cathedral. "Among the Peers of the Realm, you know my lance to be without peer."

That braggart always has to let everyone know, thought Abhoc. *As if he doesn't get twice the practice time of anyone else.*

"Choose me, Lord Brum," growled Abhoc. "To no danger's daunt shall I ever yield."

Danger's daunt? mouthed Heckley back at him. Abhoc shrugged.

"Um, charge me, Lord Brum," said Bubo feebly, "to do the, uh, air-charging. A-horse."

The knight commander allowed Bubo a pregnant moment to feel stupid.

"Sir Heckleham of Newarkshire!" Brum then bellowed. "Summon your strength and ready your arms. For the High King Harthur prefers his clubs *without* onions."

The revelers *oooohed* the sick burn.

"I'm no sandwich technician," said Abhoc (though that was totally his day job), "but I say onions don't belong on clubs at all."

Like an arrow, Brum fired his burning gaze across the gap, striking the Pestilence's greatest pest between the eyes. A smoldering countenance answered him, fire-for-fire.

"They sure don't," Brum scowled.

"But you don't have a ramp," someone called from the crowd.

"We don't need a ramp," answered Brum. "Heckley's horse can clear it."

"M'lord," said Heckley quietly, "it is unchivalrous not to prepare a landing zone for thy opponent in the sky joust."

"Then don't let him live long enough to land!" barked Brum.

"M'Lord," repeated Heckley, disapprovingly.

Spewing a volley of Middle German that would have made a fair damsel blush, Brum slipped down from his saddle. From under his Teutonic helm, hair flowed and fell to his shoulders. "Laser shield," he said. A pentagon of blue light appeared on his leather bracer. Tattooed across his shoulders sprawled the portrait of a lion, the wild mane encircling its regal head like a halo, the noble snout tinged with blood. The musculature of man and beast alike was lean and powerful.

The knight commander set himself, crouching slightly. The lion seemed to roar as Brum exploded toward the wall, leading with his shoulder. His hips snapped forward, bringing the shield hard to bear against the stone. Brum pushed, the sinew in his neck straining, the might of his calves and quads driving him like a wedge between tower and turret, until the century-old masonry, having withstood sieges and engines of war, groaned like a dying elephant. The mortar surrendered. As continents split, driven apart by tectonic forces, so too the old stones fractured and fell, ringing one against the other as they tumbled from the battlement, nine stories to the moat below. Only a foot of rubble remained.

The laser shield on Brum's wrist flickered and died, its power depleted.

As the stones splashed in the murky water, Heckley's mare, sensing what was about to happen, began to shy.

Her rider, about to swear up a blue streak, took a deep breath instead.

"Oh, don't be that way, Potato Chip," Heckley said, cooing in her ear. "You're a brave girl! Look at you, not afraid of heights. You're not afraid of the cwazy purple man's sizzle stick neither! No. So a little water's not going to spook you now. Is it, my pretty pegasus?"

Abhoc removed his helmet and scratched his head bashfully.

"Sometimes I ask myself why we didn't just build a supertank," he admitted to the crowd.

This got a bit of a laugh.

"Easy now, m'Lady To-Chip." Heckley had dismounted to pet his mare's cheek.

Sensing what was going on, the crowd began to murmur. Abhoc decided to entertain the masses during the delay. He switched to his mountain accent, which city folk found so charming.

"When we first trained ourselves of chivalry 'n what, horses came scarce, so we rode on what came. A year ago, we singled on mares. Ask why. A stallion won't let a turbo thruster anywhere near his, y'know, netherworld. Nor care to fly! The ladies braver, s'true. But myself I sympathize with the gentlemen's point of view. Not all ches'nuts want an open fire."

A few of the party-goers smiled woodenly, fearful that the big show may have ended before it started.

"Listen, don't get me wrong. 'Tween Hoofmary here and my own wife, this one's got the more 'greeable temperament. But afore we set ourselves on all this techin', I says to Brum, what if we just build ourselves death-cycles. Just *call* 'em destriers or chargers. Name bikes for horses, like they do with cars. Paint 'em with checkerboards and chess pieces. People'll see how's we're Horselords on the rise again. Only but now for an age of machines. No feed bags, no dung heaps. We can even make 'em electrical. Ecological, ya know? Quiet. No bad smells at all. Best of all, death-cycles ain't shy of no damn water."

Abhoc's audience laughed politely, but their eyes fixed across the gap. The Purple Onion was arguing with a man in a rhinestone top hat how best to reinforce a hubcap and fit it to his forearm.

"Oh no worry of the Onion over there," he said. "Realizes now he needs a shield or ol' Heckley will kill him outright. Run him through like a melon atop a post. That's how we practice, by a'way. Melon posts. A few years ago, some American came over and said, ''Ey, what're you doing? You're driving up overhead on my act.' We asked what he needed so mucho melonos for. 'Comedy,' he says. Comedy! Well, what's the joke, we ask. 'Broken melons,' says him. Don't get it, me. A broken head, sure, is funny. Broken what else, not so much."

150

Nothing. Not a titter. Abhoc tried again.

"I like the artistry of the joust, you know. The sacred war ritual. Reunite with your Tectonic roots, all that. But give me pitchéd battle any day. Or a bar fight. 'N one man try to kill another, there's simplicity. Jus' grab a bottle and start swinging. But two men *agree* to kill each other, aw, now it's about production value. The natural act of murder, forget it: now you got, uh, director, producer, scrip' writer, prop manager. 'Cause here's what you gotta have: First, the saying of proud words. Rrrrrr!, all that. Then you gotta make bicker on the terms. 'Cause if you don' can't find something wrong, you ain't done it before. Means 'r an amateur. Green from the garden gets you green in the grave. That done, find a pen. For versification. 'My dear might'r-be widow, if you readin' this,' all that. Big quill feather fluffin' over 'r shoulder. But hold still, not yet. Never a man knows his business till come time to put a lance through a man's head. Now remembers candles need ordering for his daughter's quinceañera. Now remembers 'as a daughter. Ol' Heck here got two. Both fairer lookin' than the father, I thank God. Whoever he is."

Abhoc licked his lips. "The father, not God, I mean. God is His Majesty, J. Harthur Christ."

He noticed Heckley had given up trying to sweet talk his mare, and was now rubbing some kind of ointment on her gums.

"Then all that done," Abhoc said, "you still gotta drug your fucking horse!"

He smiled friendly, with all the teeth he could manage. The

crowd was lukewarm, at best. *These duddies better get entertained soon,* he thought, *or I'm gonna start cutting some new laugh holes.*

•

An equine-mounted propulsion system and cling wrap body armor had been game changers for the Pestilence, but the true genius of the Church's R&D team was a jousting lance for modern urban warfare. Made of a titanium/aluminum alloy, it was lightweight and flexible, yet durable enough to skewer three skulls on a single pass. Heckley had tested it on hundreds of materials and knew a direct hit would pierce right through the Onion's makeshift shield. Even a glancing blow would throw him from the bike, nine fatal stories above the asphalt.

Every muscle in Heckley's body was prepared for this joust. Once they'd established their trajectories, he could hit the target with his eyes closed.

"For luck," said a woman's voice.

He turned. Her lace-trimmed dress seemed years out of style, and driblets of mascara stained her cheeks. And wasn't she too old for clubbing? *But Dodoville can age a person so fast,* he thought.

She held out something to him, hung limply between her fingers. The other arm twisted nervously behind her back.

The danger he faced now excited many of the party-goers, but this woman seemed genuinely afraid for him, about to make a death-defying pass against a known predator.

"Don't worry," he said smiling. "If a man alive can best me at the joust, he's not in Dodoville tonight."

Her foot brushed the back of her ankle. She twitched indecisively, her hand still out, words dying unformed on her lips.

Tightening his grip on the reins, Heckley lowered himself to accept the trinket and offer his cheek for a kiss. In a sudden flurry, she flung her arms around him. She was sobbing—more like screaming in his ear!

He studied her face again. No, their paths had never crossed.

"By your honor, m'lady," he said jovially, disentangling himself. "I'll soon have that rapscallion sorted."

He didn't know if this sounded courtly, but it did the trick. Reassured, she sniffled and laughed shyly. Three shrill little shrieks. With a bow, she scampered away.

Heckley looked at the handkerchief. It was a pinkish cream color, embroidered with an evergreen motif. He had owned one just like it once, though he couldn't think why. His instincts urged him to throw it away.

As their eyes met again, she glanced down and smiled.

He stuffed it into one of his leather bracers.

The narcotic he'd given Potato Chip was quick acting: his mare already saw the Onion as something she'd like to gnash apart with her teeth.

Across the gap, Heckley's adversary was posing for photographs with the crowd. Nothing about that purple moron's bearing betrayed he had only moments to live.

The lion must confront even the hare with all its strength, Heckley reminded himself.

It was a pity they would not meet in hand-to-hand combat: sword against quarterstaff was Heckley's favorite melee pairing, and rumor had it that the Onion was a worthy opponent. But at least Dodoville would witness them fighting across the sky. Like gods.

Heckley watched the Onion fit the motorcycle helmet over his mask. Two gold points of light shone behind the visor. An illusion of the night, it must be. Or perhaps an onboard AI? No matter. Heckley's equipment was optimized for the task at hand, balance strength and reach.

Once the Onion was dead, Heckley would unmask him. Anticlimactic, whoever it was. Life had taught him if you wore a monk's habit to confiscate people's property, or if you pretended to be a knight so you could crush some skulls, these became your true faces. The same for someone who dressed as a vegetable to act out his messiah complex. The person out of costume became the real disguise.

Heckley recognized the handkerchief now, from one of his jobs for the Archive. Christ's spurs, that scientist!

About a year ago, an anonymous foreign investor had issued the Consortium a special request for an exiled botanist living in Dodoville. Anyone on earth can do bad math, Heckley had thought, but somebody wanted this guy special. To put in a display case, for all he knew. He and his partner had boxed and labeled that lab monkey like a regular artifact. They left a receipt for him on the kitchen counter, like he were a teapot or something.

Strange as the affair had been, he might have forgotten it except for the fuss the man raised. If only Heckley would find a way to lose him, the scientist promised anything within his power, nothing too precious or too sordid. Life simply didn't exist for him outside of Dodoville, he said. Untenable, simply untenable.

Heckley assumed it was empty talk. But on the morning the buyer was to collect the goods, they found him dead in his storage locker. He had wrapped the damn handkerchief around his neck and twisted the ends till he choked himself. Bulging eyeballs and embroidered evergreens.

How odd, Heckley remembered thinking. In Dodoville, you teetered every day at the brink of destruction—itself a kind of death. He'd always imagined being delivered from here would be like being reborn.

Heckley led his mare to the launch point. He accepted well wishes on either side of his saddle, clasping hands and returning the high salutes which some revelers assumed knights like him must make. When they asked to stroke his mustaches, he grinned and swore on his lance that he'd run them through if they tried.

Across the gap, the Onion was enduring his own love fest, chuckling at those who shed crocodile tears at his approach, dislocating the shoulder of someone to tried to remove his mask. (He popped it back in to show no hard feelings.)

Both here and atop the garage, everyone cheered the warrior in their own midst. Club Towers for Sir Heckley. Across the way, Team Onion. If any breast housed a deeper allegiance than this, they kept it to themselves.

Heckley thought about those samurai movies where the two warriors whose loyalties had crossed set out into the wilderness together before dawn. They walked in file, the silence between them noble, intimate, with a touch of the sacred. Qualities he had always lacked in his own life. They reached the designated place as the sun broke upon the horizon. The adversaries faced each other and bowed, the strong wind that whipped their kimonos the only sign of the turmoil inside. No witnesses to the duel but their honor. They fought, sword clanging upon sword. When one had slain the other, the victor bowed again and closed his opponent's eyes. The two departed, one in body, one in spirit. The only sound the wailing wind.

Ah, bliss.

About him now, riotous voices. "Heck-El-Ham. Heck-El-Ham." This idiotic emBritishment of his name hadn't existed until Bubo uttered it earlier today.

Around the Purple Onion, a different chant had gone up. Only when actors mimed it out did Heckley understand the words: *Kill the horse. Kill the horse.*

On this side, Heckley's crowd, having touched and smelled the mythic monster, identified with its fearsome power. Over there, the mare was an abomination that needed to be destroyed.

Poor Potato Chip had to land in hostile territory! Heckley

156

petted his mare on the neck and enabled her self-defense appliances. *Poor those folks.*

All was ready. Abhoc stood by the retaining wall with a flare gun. When it exploded over the gap, that was the signal to charge. Abhoc raised a hand to silence the crowds. Heckley heard the Onion Chopper's engine turn over. His own thrusters came to life.

The gun fired. The flare popped. Heckley spurred his horse.

Spectators who leaned over the runway to watch his approach got sucked closer by the vacuum of his passing. The terrible hoofbeats devoured the roof. He reached the wall and his mare leaped, hind legs trailing like a comet's tail as an explosion from the thrusters carried forward rider and mount.

Heckley saw the yellow flash of the Onion's lance, the purple blur of the motorcycle, the chrome circle of his useless buckler.

For an instant, the silence he craved enveloped him, borne aloft by eternity.

He felt the handkerchief stuffed under his bracer blow loose into the night.

The scientist had died for her, he realized, the mousy woman with mascara on her cheeks who had fallen in love with him just now. His head turned slightly to catch sight of it floating away.

For half an instant, he let his lance fall.

Not accused, yet condemned by her kiss, judge and jury in the smallness of a world where fragments of the past always came back to you. He felt everything escape with that tear-soaked rag, snatched from him by an invisible hand.

At once, the judgment of God was upon him, striking him like a thunderbolt. The electricity of it struck his chest and burned him to his extremities. As the abyss enveloped him, he saw the tiny square of cloth against the veil of night.

Vengeance on the wind, embroidered with evergreen trees.

•

As the quarterstaff struck, spectators saw the knight's body rise from the saddle as if lifted by the arms of an angel, then fall as if crushed by the archangel's hammer. A crackling cascade of sparks chased the limp form down from the dome of heaven, the slumped shoulders catching flame like a meteor. The body struck the moat around Club Towers, raising a tsunami of swill and filth that overflowed its banks then receded into lapping waves. Bubbles rose and died.

The riderless mare completed the pass and landed deftly on the makeshift ramp upon the parking garage. The tailgaters, who moments ago had clamored for her death, fell silent in awe.

Heavy as a monument, light-moving as a breeze, the regal animal trotted into their midst, her eyes and mouth glowing a hellish red. She snorted, expelling deep-colored smoke from her nostrils.

A standoff: one demon versus a multitude of mortals.

A shot rang out from the crowd. Kertwang! The animal kicked, terrifying her assailants with the endless pink expanse of her tongue and gums. As more reports followed, a hideous whinnying laughter seemed summoned up from below. The volley intensified until it faded at last into impotent clinks.

As Potato Chip stomped a steel hoof, sparks flew from the concrete. Smoke from her nostrils swirled blue and purple.

One woman stepped forward. "Don't be fooled by superstition," she cried. "A horse is not a monster! Or a demon! It is a creature of nature, which humans domesticated thousands of years ago. Like dogs and cats! So there's no reason to be afraid. If we act with authority, it will obey us!"

A silence followed.

"You go get it, then!" someone yelled.

The woman ventured a step forward. And another. The creature of nature stiffened but suffered her approach. A tentative hand reached out to pet the roan snout. The mare's breathing eased as froth dribbled from her lip.

Slowly, the great head bowed.

Sensing a gesture of submission, the woman advanced to take the reins.

Twin plumes of fire belched from nozzles in the bridle. The woman screamed and leaped back. The mare reared up, a cyclone of hooves spinning before her. She came down hard, horseshoes popping on the concrete like firecrackers.

Once again, the horse lowered her head deeply and scraped the ground with her hoof.

The woman looked to the crowd, uncomprehending.

Again, fire spewed from the creature's maw. Again she reared and pawed the air and bowed and scraped the ground. Eyes afire, she took a step closer.

Knowing better than to show the beast her back and run but too terrified to do anything else, the woman fell to her knees and pressed her forehead against the ground.

Potato Chip neighed and nodded her head in approval. Then she turned to the next person.

Who needed no further encouragement. He too knelt and bowed.

Like a wave, the entire crowd prostrated themselves before the magnificent creature and begged for mercy.

Graciously, Potato Chip acquiesced as she waited patiently for her master.

•

The crowd atop Club Towers that had leaned forward to watch the knight pass now jumped back to allow the motorcycle to stick its landing, veins of neon pumping purplish light across the chassis. The Onion's sizzle stick crackled as he hoisted it triumphantly above his head like a thunderbolt.

There just wasn't enough runway.

The Onion leaped backward from his seat in a slender arc, like a knife flipped blade over pommel, as the chopper skidded out into the retaining wall. He landed lightly on one knee, holding out the quarterstaff parallel to the ground, like a missive scroll from the land of grievous beatings.

Brum nodded to Abhoc, who lowered his lance and charged. The Onion jumped up, quarterstaff battering the lance to one side, catching the mare on the jaw with the backswing, then again on her flank as she passed. The horse's spider-silk armor dispersed the physical blow, but the electrical contact echoed like a transformer box exploding. It took all of Abhoc's skill to keep the animal from throwing him.

For reasons beyond anyone's comprehension, DJ Skymole was playing Fleetwood Mac.

"Maim and murder as you will, Lord Brum," said the Onion, his voice even but authoritative. "You'll carry no booty home to your profane church tonight!"

"So many times now," the knight commander replied, "you've made citizens of Dodoville blubber their most shameful secrets before the entire city—but this time it is you who shall be the spectacle. I've lured you here, out into the heart of the Saturday night. Now tens of thousands of honorable Horsefolk, to whom this territory has always belonged, will be shown that you are just another agent of the ganglords, who for the last century have sought to abolish our culture, denigrate our heroes, and deny our God-given rights of plunder. But we Pestilence shall prove even an Onion can be beat."

"Get it, beet?" muttered Abhoc to no one at all.

Brum's war hammer, basically a steel breeze block on a mahogany handle, swung down upon the Onion's head, its arc

161

shredding the moonlight into tattered ribbons of color. The Onion braced his quarterstaff and received the blow. The clang reverberated as pure as silver on gold, while Stevie Nicks adored or implored the names of Sara or Rhiannon or whoever.

As the Onion struggled to regain his feet, Abhoc lowered his sword and attempted to slash out the throat from under his mask.

A battle so fierce followed, even the indifferent gods who molder beneath the clay earth raised a stony eye to watch.

•

A horse is not a dragon. If you ride one off a tower, you will surely die. Right? Mandi knew nothing about war but she knew that.

Death seemed such a lonely thing, so she had given the knight a token to keep him company in his last moments. She could think of nothing worse than this—than thinking of someone dying alone!

With her handkerchief on his wrist, even his senseless death could be for something, she thought. In the stories she'd tell, it would be.

Once upon a time, she had believed in chivalry: the romance of my lady fair with whose blessing you rode into battle, trusting love to conquer all.

But in the end, she learned, only death wins. The only conqueror is death.

The flare of the starter's pistol had exploded above the gap.

His lance and helmet and shield, all polished and laser-y. The revelers' tongues' parched for a dewdrop of destiny. How important it all looked, this heavy-hooved action!

She watched his colors trail after him into the annihilating night. She forced herself to see a beautiful thing in this. Still, he was dying for nothing. At least, now he died for nothing *for her*.

Farewell. This time she had gotten to meep out her goodbye. Even if it had been to a stranger.

High in that hanging void of darkness now crackled a ball of orange light, opening like a portal from the future. Out spat that veiny Onion Chopper. The purple-glowing machine hurled past, nearly clipping her up and crushing her against the masonry wall—as it had that nice, attractive couple standing next to her.

This was pain renewing its assault on her. It would persist in hunting her until she was dead. And then keep after her, probably.

Mandi stood, feeling nothing.

Voices spoke. They chimed like a bell, or ground like a stone. Through the sliver of her eyelids, she saw a fog in which an ocean of dark crashed against a shore of light.

Animal stink mingled with machine exhaust as petty gods disputed around her. Staves, darts, and bolos answered axes, spears, and swords. So many weapons for only a handful of actors! As if pulled from invisible pockets, or the arsenal of their enormous personas.

Imperiled bystanders scurried for their lives but showed no

sign of departing. The air thickened with scraps of evening wear or pieces of nose from intoxicated fools who stumbled when they should have staggered.

One party-goer's skull exploded in front of her. She didn't even see from what.

Mandi felt the urge to step into the fracas and fight for Sven. For his safety, his future happiness, for the great gifts he still had to offer the world. But what eye might she blacken, what spleen rupture or kneecap pulverize, that could add anything to his joy or worth? He had vanished forever to that unknown country, which was probably Death and not Peru. Yet every moment that passed, she felt the opportunity escaping, and she cursed herself for her cowardice.

For a year now, she had cast no shadow because the light shone through her. In photographs, her face looked like an unfinished drawing. Far too often, she found it impossible to tell if costumers in her shop where speaking to her or themselves. Like a ghost, she was prone to slamming doors and breaking things just to prove she existed at all.

Mandi had no idea what this battle was over, what would change if one side succumbed to the other. But in Dodoville, fights seldom required a meaning or object. Hers was a city of furies, demonic remnants from past ages who remembered nothing of life except they had been wronged in it. The Pestilence for instance: how did people who burned down houses for a living believe they had been mistreated? But here they were now to settle a score. Also, the Purple Onion: surely his actions, too, were held in fief to some egregious suffering.

(Her best guess, an aggravated case of survivor guilt. Where else could he have picked up the idiot notion that he could not die?)

Had . . . someone just hurled a trident past her?

But if furies could arise to avenge long-dead plunderers or . . . whatever vegetal trauma the Purple Onion had endured, where was the bright-colored revenant of how *she* had suffered? Why wasn't *it* handing out drubbings upon this rooftop?

Mandi watched the Onion clobber the shit out of the red knight with the sassy mouth. So fast did the quarterstaff spin and prod, jab and pound, sometimes Abhoc fell from a blow she hadn't even seen. By tomorrow, his whole body ought to be a mottle of colors.

In the last year, she had built her whole life around grief, but standing now like a child amid this storm of violence, she felt it coming apart in a landslide. *It's time,* she thought, wringing her hands. *Time to bring it down.*

•

The broken battleaxe clattered on the ground as Abhoc crashed to his knees. Ghoulish in defeat, his eyes showed mostly white, his hair aflame with tongues of electricity.

Early on, the knight had fought admirably, but his damaged jaw required protection at all costs, and the Onion was able to pick open holes in Abhoc's defenses. Quick, restrained strikes rained down over his body, exhausting the muscles with shocks and bruising the flesh with blows. A death of a thousand cuts.

(Except, of course, with beatings.)

The spectators cringed as Abhoc fell forward onto his face. His body twitched but did not stir.

Was it over now? asked Stevie Nicks, a tinge of taunt in her voice.

The Onion's yellow glove ran over Abhoc's scalp and hoisted him up by the hair to squat on his hams. The jaw hung open. Blood gushed from a newly-broken nose. The Onion lay the end of his quarterstaff at Abhoc's throat as if it were a blade.

"Why do you make riot against these people?" the Onion asked soothingly. "Tell me how pride in your sins has led you to error."

"He must be dead," someone observed. "No one takes a beating like that and keeps breathing."

The Onion shook his head. "The soul may not depart before it offers me a complete confession."

"Look, bro," came the reply, "You look like a guy who's used to getting people to do what you say. But not this time."

Pinpricks of light flashed in the vigilante's eyes. "While mortals sleep, others broker deals with the Dread Lord Death himself," he said, "who has decreed *this* the hour for wailing and gnashing of teeth."

"I'm not salty, dude," said the critic. "That asshole's just hacked off my nostril with his freakin' flail. I'm just saying. That good knight's gone none too gentle."

With his thumb, the Onion caressed Abhoc's cheek below the orbits of the eyes and tears began to flow. Bubbles of air burbled up in the blood upon the mouth.

"The weight of your crimes lies heavy upon you," said the Onion, "but I have freed your heart to relieve that burden. Speak. Simply speak and your sins will give voice of their own accord. Allow the words to pour forth and absolve you of iniquity."

Near the far wall, seated high in his saddle, Brum snarled. So far in this battle, the knight commander had gotten no worse than he'd given, but now he was seizing the opportunity for a breather. "Sir Abhoc has withstood tortures even a sadist like you cannot imagine. My Lord Rutabaga, he cannot be broken. Expect no satisfaction from him."

"Nonsense." The purple mask moved close enough to brush the hair by Abhoc's ear. "Let go. I have given you the power to end your suffering."

Abhoc's lungs forced out a tender wail.

"Use your words, Sir Abhoc," said the Onion.

"I wanted them to like me!" he whimpered.

The crowd inhaled with audible wonder.

Abhoc's voice had resounded clearly over the rooftop: the quarterstaff under his chin contained an amplifier.

"When I was growing up in New Guernsey," he said,

"everyone was always beating up anybody different: the smart kid, the one who played the tuba, the one whose family worshiped spiders. Hell, once I got my head kicked off 'cause my socks almost matched. Deserved it too, acting like I was pleet enough to buy 'em in pairs."

In Abhoc's lap, fingernails picked at bruised knuckles as he continued shamefully.

"Till then, I'd felt the world always pressuring me to make a big crumb of myself, be my own best sod. Whereas all I'd wanted was to be a reg'lar piece a shit like my pops. 'Cause really, ain't that enough? Instead of acting like I'ms a shelf up from wheres I'm at."

With tears pouring down his cheeks, hair maybe a tiny bit on fire, Abhoc cut a pathetic figure. Onlookers smiled sadly.

"And maybe it was just the fat nog o' me hurting so bad, but that's when the light shone through. And thought here's my calling. I'd like to be like a bodhisattva, goading 'em good folks down the way to ordinary shit-sackery. Let learn 'em want to want not. Not to strabe and err. I'd vowed *to pound that wisdom in* like was pounded in mine, with the blunt end. Till all's too small and frightened for the err of pride."

Abhoc's right hand gathered up fistfuls of air from the ground and collected them in the crook of his elbow.

"What I come for today, it's for those reg'lar shit sacks like me, to bust some room open for that one day when they too can get ahead, where they too can stand up and treat others like garbage, like all else treat them. 'Cause now, some people will never be beautiful, never be talented, never be smart or creative. But is that reason they can't be better than someone else? I wanted to show all the reg'lar sacks of shit, yes you *can* get to treat people worse than garbage, that's a right God-given. But you gotta be willin' a-stand up and don't let no laws tell what you're right to do!"

The crowd nodded approvingly to each other. *Where do laws get off, really, telling you what's the worst you can be to someone?*

"I'm tired of a world where heroes are always mutants and rejects and the accident-prone. Some half man, half ninja spud. Are you saying we gotta work on our *weird* to matter? Those born a quality of nothing wrong shouldn't have to always prove it, every year, every month, every damn day—not like some of 'em Quasimodos do. Amn't I a given? Shouldn't I get to be? Listen, I'm not even Horsefolk, just a reg'lar don't-know-where-the-fuck-I'm-from. But the fact I'm here, showing I got a right for a horse to bear me—"

Bravo. You are definitely here, sir knight, that's a fact!

"Where was I? Listen, here's truth for one and all. It's ordinary folks the real ones being ostrapated, who ain't even got their own rights to burn and pillage anymore. Tchotchke merchants and botanists and drama nerds, in this town they can shit wherever they want, but never real people like who make sandwiches. Who have to say, no, of course, I'll make it again with less mustard, when that customer can't even handle a mace or flail."

169

That's true. Why do we even have *weapons if not to say who gets treated politely?*

"All I want, all I really ask, is when some grouchy ol' cigarillo screams at me, And where's my pickle! I can clock her nog off, just for the manners. No apologies! Instead of, Oh saws, you getta cookie, an' an' an' . . ."

Abhoc's broken body, till now replete with verbiage, seemed able to go no further.

"And what, Sir Abhoc?" said the Purple Onion. "Unburden yourself this holdback and be free at last. What of the cookie?"

The red knight squealed. "An' it comes outta my pay!"

The crowd gasped.

Brum, too, let his head fall to his chest and squeezed shut his eyes in shame.

The Onion let go of Abhoc's hair. The knight collapsed in a heap, sobbing. "It comes outta my pay!" he repeated.

All around them, the gentle applause of emotional support.

"There there, Sir Abhoc," said the Onion. "Nicely done."

"I don't even cry when I cut onions!" he sniffed. A bashful laugh escaped him as his vanquisher clasped him warmly on the shoulder.

•

Victor Cumin stood triumphant as party-goers whistled and cheered around him.

It comes outta my pay.

From a psychological standpoint, he saw how the lifelong degradation of menial employment had left this man little recourse but to acquire state-beyond-the-art equestrian warfare technology and terrorize ravers at an '80s party. It all made sense now.

As acting president of the Cumin Media news conglomerate, the result of tonight's lacrimation ritual pleased him. Usually, when the Violet Storm beat a criminal within an inch of death, the story that person spat up never made much sense. In order for the video go viral on social media, it usually had to rely on the victim's physical abasement, the pathetic facial expression, and, above all, the mucus. Nothing stimulated advertisers' cash flow like nose flow. (His clue had been when he found a website offering analyses of the snot bubbles: estimated booger size, viscosity, all that.)

"Thank you, Purple Onion" whimpered Abhoc. "Thank you."

The defeated knight held out a hand from where he lay on the ground. Victor grasped it to thunderous applause. Even the marauder's steed put forward a hoof and bowed in homage. *That'll play great on Instagram!* he thought.

On that roof, dozens of videos were being live-streamed to the web. Naturally, the feed from his own body camera would provide Cumin Media's official HD version of Abhoc's bloody face.

"I don't really understand why I'm crying," the knight said. "I felt worse from the hangover I had this morning."

Everybody laughed. After a night of being held hostage by rodeo clowns in medieval makeup, the joke bled some of the tension out of the air.

"When I look at you," Abhoc began.

Victor was holding Abhoc's head by the badly bruised jaw so it was impossible for him to look away from his camera.

"When I look into your face, such as it is, I feel as if I'm gazing into the nexus of the universe, from which everything issues and everything returns. Not that it's impossible to lie, per se. Only there wouldn't be any point."

"Will you make war on Dodoville again?" Victor asked.

"Never," said Abhoc, "not for all my days."

"Do you swear?"

"By my lance and Christ's spurs," Abhoc intoned, "I do swear."

What choice does he have? thought Victor with satisfaction. Before the hundred or so present tonight and the thousands more who would see it online, Abhoc had wept like a ninny over the cookie he was forced to buy for a customer in a sandwich shop. Abhoc's strength was broken. If he went around bashing brains out now, no Dodovillean worth their salt wouldn't die laughing at him.

"All for nothing," thundered Brum suddenly.

As the quarterstaff lay across Victor's knee, Brum's enormous destrier, practically a horse and a half, stomped on the extruding length and snapped it in half, leaving Victor with the short end, divorced from its electric power generator.

"Well, that's rude," he said.

Brum drew his sword. "This has been all too cute, Parsnip! But now it ends." The knight commander raised the weapon above his head and made ready to bring down the death blow.

Victor felt Abhoc's hands tighten around his right thumb, holding him in place. A small giggle escaped from the bloodied mouth.

Huh, Victor thought. *I wonder how I'm going to get out of this one.*

•

The broken quarterstaff skittered across the ground to Mandi's feet. The shaft's light had died but electricity still crackled from the jagged end. She picked it up without thinking, like a delivery left at her doorstep. It felt significant in her hand, and she held it like a stick for writing messages on the beach. Here I Am, Here I Have Tread. For a few hours, the groove of the letters would declare her significance to the cosmos before the sea washed them away.

She looked up. Lord Brum and the Purple Onion seemed seconds from settling their dispute. Whoever won, not much would change. Violent and perverse actions like this would still govern Dodoville's future. Might as well root for whoever had the better costume! Because for people like her, nothing really mattered more than the aesthetics.

Only. Maybe this time it was different. Perhaps, for once, it had fallen to her to be an author instead of a reader of the madness in tomorrow's headlines?

Like a thunderbolt, the quarterstaff fragment pulsed in her hand.

What would that mean to her, to make some sort of difference?

In a sense, it was as much as she could ever hope for.

Closing her eyes, she lunged with the broken staff, her whole body behind the blow.

When Mandi thought back on it later, she did not remember deciding whom to strike. She watched the jagged end of the staff slide between flap where the horse's hood overhung its body armor. She felt the apparatus pierce the flesh, she winced as it scraped past bone and penetrated what she assumed was the heart. As the staff injected raw energy into living flesh, she swore her fingers could feel that muscle start and stop a thousand times as the jolt arrested the towering animal.

Finally, the power source overloaded, and Brum's terrifying steed collapsed, toasted like a campfire marshmallow. It was all Brum could do not to be crushed under his behemoth mount as it fell.

For Mandi, time stopped and rewound. It played out a bit, paused for a snack, checked its email real quick. When life started up again, she'd sorta forgot what was happening. But she smelled roasted horse hair. She saw Brum stagger over to Abhoc's only slightly traumatized mare and pull himself up on her back. He slapped the reins and headed for the ramp that spiraled down the tower.

Gradually, she noticed the Purple Onion was staring at her instead of his escaping adversary, that the broken quarterstaff was no longer in her hands but his. Once again, she paused and rewound time. On this pass, she saw him twist away from the prod she'd aimed at the small of this back, she watched indifferently as he redirected her stolen momentum at Brum's destrier and saved himself from an otherwise inevitable beheading.

This strange man in the purple jumpsuit and—wait, were those fuzzy slippers he was wearing?—she had tried to kill him. Why?

Behind the mask, he was studying her face. She felt herself giving everything away inside her as if it were written there.

At first, she'd tried to turn away, but now she wished she could see and read it too.

Would-be Onion slayer. Was that her? Was that the real Mandi-in-her-bones, in her reptile brain?

"My child," the man in the mask said, his voice eerily calm.

Mandi fell to her knees. The camera was just above the insignia on his chest. (Was it supposed to be hidden? Who was he fooling?) She looked directly into it now. The tears began to well up in her eyes.

"It was a year ago," she began. "We were out of garlic for the pesto."

The Onion crushed her head gently against his body.

"Hush, my child. This is not for you."

Is he trying to comfort me? she thought.

In any case, his embrace darkened out the video feed.

"But I tried to kill you," she muttered. "I was about to jam that rod right up your purple asshole!"

"Shh, shh. The danger is passed."

Mandi's voice shook. "I deserve this. I *earned* this."

"Psh, psh. Don't you see? The storm is over. You deserve nothing. Nothing at all."

Mandi tried to shove him back, to get eyes on his fucking camera. His grip remained iron.

"It was a year ago," she stammered again. It took all her courage to speak. "I went out to get garlic for the pesto!"

Letting go, the Onion pressed his cheek to the top of her head and wandered off to salvage his Chopper.

Mandi remained on her knees. She was shaking with rage. "It was a year ago!" she screamed at his back. "We were out. Of fucking. Garlic!"

Who needed him? She had witnesses right here. All around her.

Mandi lifted her head, but no one paid her any attention. The dead horse had mesmerized them.

Stretched across the ground, it seemed even larger now, legs thick as a man's, nostrils as wide as oranges, somehow more invincible-looking than it had in life. The newly fallen body of a tyrannosaurus or an archangel could not have held them more in rapture, not for the size nor silenced danger.

Mandi too felt herself fall under its thrall. *Until this moment, I had lived in an age of wonders*, she thought.

Gazing at the proud creature struck down, she felt as distant as the rest. Somehow this was not her work. She had no hand. In this or anything.

Her story died in her throat. The words refused to form. The tears didn't come.

Time restarted.

Around her, a flurry of movement. People attended on the wounded, the dead, and the dying. Searchlights from helicopters shone upon the roof, mussing well-styled coiffures as they hovered closer. Red and blue lights of cop cars flashed in a perimeter down below. Mandi had almost forgotten the police could exist! Journalists from the *Spyhole* and the *Inquisitor* interviewed patrons on the scene. Barbacks swept up broken glass and severed limbs, mopping away the booze and blood. A thousand things were transpiring at once.

None of them were happening to Mandi. No one was looking at her. No one was listening. She was completely alone.

•

From his DJ station near the retaining wall, Bubo took stock of the aftermath of the Pestilence's assault. Two knights defeated, the third fled. Witnesses innumerable. The stamp of the Purple Onion everywhere.

Down below, he saw emergency personnel had dragged

Heckley from the moat and were administering medical attention.

"Turn the music off, please!" came a voice over a megaphone.

Bubo turned up the volume. All these screaming people were making it hard to think.

The drawbridge lowered over the moat, and Brum crossed over on Abhoc's horse. A trio of police officers waited for him. Brum pointed up at the top of the tower.

His voice was transmitting over Bubo's headset.

"The Purp is still up there," said the knight commander. "He busted in without even showing identification! For a half hour now, he's been murdering and mayheming at an otherwise peaceful rave. We fought him as best we could, but there's a pile of bodies as tall as you are. If you hurry now, you might still apprehend him!"

The officers consulted each other.

"Do you have a license to operate that class H vehicle?" one asked.

Brum ignited his booster and trampled over them. As he sped away, officers opened fire, but the shots deflected harmlessly off the mare's red spider silk body armor.

"Hey Bob," said a voice. "Bob! The show's over already."

Bubo noticed the Purple Onion had retrieved his motorcycle from where it crashed upon his landing. He'd managed to get the engine started and was performing a maintenance check. For a man whose principle adversary was escaping, for whom the cops were closing in, he seemed in no particular hurry. What a weirdo.

"Fuck's sake, Bob! Turn that racket off."

A small balding man in a bartender's polo was standing in front of him.

Bubo powered down his station. "Hi boss," he said meekly.

"Bob, you promised if I let you DJ tonight you'd bring the best crowd this club has ever seen. I didn't believe you, but this is always a slow weekend, so I gave you a chance."

"I know, boss," said Bubo, "and I know what you are going to say, but you can't buy publicity like this. Tonight's gonna—"

"Can't buy, Bob?" said the owner. "You telling me I can't just *buy* four murderers and a catastrophuck? I can't go *down to the murderer and catastrophuck store* and buy myself the shitshow I had me tonight? I wonder why that is, Bob."

"There's no need to be snarky, sir. It kinda hurts my feelings."

"Oh, your feelings? Maybe it was protecting your feelings that no one's offered to kill and maim all my customers for me. As a service to modest businessmen like myself, who's worried he's been making just too much fucking money!"

Bubo's horse hung her head and pawed sadly at the ground.

The Onion Chopper's engine roared to life. Its rider kicked the bike into gear and charged the gap Brum had broken into the retaining wall. The vehicle fell about three stories before the neon gravity thrusters came to life and lay it down softly behind the police barricade. It disappeared down the street Brum had taken.

"God damn it," cried one of the officers on the ground. "That's the second time today!"

"You're fired, Bob," said the owner quietly. "You'll never DJ in Dodoville again."

"The CKE can help you recoup—"

The owner silenced him with a smack on the cheek. "Not because you wrecked my club. Your playlist is fucking weak. I got a goddamn sword fight on my roof, and you're playing that witchy shit!"

"What did you want?" cried Bubo. "Choral music in Latin? That's so cliche!"

"Oh, we got the avant-garde here! Hey everybody, it's Philip fucking Glass on a horse! Pack your gear and get out. I don't want to see your face again."

Robert Schyman aka Sir Bubo Skymole retracted his music table back into his saddle console. Gathering up his reins, he gave the scene one last look around.

"The Church of the Knight Errant has fought valiantly," he declared. "And although they did not carry the day, one thing's for sure: the Middle Ages are back, baby!"

He spurred his mare and walked her down the ramp around the outside of the tower. As he crossed the drawbridge, his eyes made a moment's contact with one of the officers sorting out the chaos on the scene.

His horse cantered out into the night.

EPISODE SIX:

THE SNIVELING IN THE SPIDERS' DEN

VICTOR SET OFF on the Storm Cycle in pursuit of Lord Brum. After his rout of the Pestilence at Club Towers, he hoped to follow the knight commander back to the CKE's hideout and break up the entire operation in one night. He just had to make sure Brum didn't know he was being tailed.

Opening a drop-down menu on his visor screen, he activated his computer's heat trail viewer. Beneath him, the street exploded into a mottled map of red, yellow, green, and blue: the energy residue of this evening's traffic. Countless streams of heavy-axled tires crisscrossed the barely perceptible etching of bicycles, the hybrid tracks of a rickshaw, and the motor treads of Percy Kaplan's grossly misnamed "street submersible." One set of horse prints.

He cut the Storm Cycle's headlight and followed. Switching

his bike to Prius mode, the engine made less noise than leaves changing color in the fall.

The charger's Equine Battle Boots(TM) headed down Soapy Smith Boulevard, hooked right past the antiques manufacturing plant, doubled backed via Unter den Zendern to the Dodos River, where they meandered a shadowy path through the vice district. The heat signature suggested a cantor. Victor instructed his bike's computer to calculate speed and match pace.

A shooting star flashed across heaven. Less than an hour ago, that had been him! But a thousand times brighter, accompanied by an explosion—and purple! Tomorrow the *Spyhole* would run a four-page spread on his meteoric descent into combat and his subsequent victory. The way he'd split the night like a thunderbolt—a force of nature!—would finally compel his writers to style him the Violet Storm. Which was good, he thought, chuckling. If one more headline called him Purple Onion, people were bound to start thinking that was his name!

On the heat viewer, the exhaust of the charger's aft thruster rose in the distance like a red sun. Brum had dismounted and hitched the animal to a parking meter, where it stretched its neck to nosh the leaves of a nearby willow tree.

The trail had led to Leper's Leap, a secluded spot on the river which had been frequented in the past by society's scorned amours. The geography of Dodoville's illicit love had since shifted, but reputedly it retained popularity with other activities trying to avoid public censure.

The shadowy willows offered his adversary too many

ambush points. Well, nowhere to go down there but the river; Brum would have to come back this way. Victor preferred to wait him out.

Shouting in the distance! A broil, metal on metal. Deploying the digital listening feature on his helmet, Victor made out voices: "Roll for initiative!" "I fear thee not, harbinger of destruction!" and "Take it thusly, catamite of the Hornèd Cockatrice!"

He really didn't want to go down there in a jumpsuit and mask—someone might ask for his armor class! Still, that was really a lot of screaming, even for dwarven blood-mages.

Slowly, with caution, Victor advanced through the willows. Probably only harmless fun.

Or Pestilence reinforcements.

He skulked a little faster, risking the snap of a dry twig or two.

By the time he neared the clearing, the tumult had fallen eerily quiet. Except for . . . Was that music?

As he stepped from behind a curtain of willow branches, the expanse of lights on the far side of the Dodos River confronted him.

At his feet, pieces of LARPing gear lay strewn across the grass, darkened with the gore of hacked-off limbs, crushed skulls, and broken necks. He counted a dozen bodies in a state that called for dental records, as if a pack of werewolves had just torn through. The battle couldn't have lasted two minutes.

Toy poleaxes, maces, and handheld trebuchets. Horace

Brumfield was a cold-blooded murderer, but this had probably been an honest mistake . . .

On the bank stood the knight commander, his foot leaning upon the concrete wall that followed the river to the sea. His batwing helmet also lay atop the barrier. As a humid breeze blew in from the water, the curls of his mullet rose and fell like waves upon his shoulder. Under his chin lay nestled his cigar box violin. His eyes were closed, his face like a babe sleeping at its mother's bosom. Hardly a splatter of gore upon him. The breath he drew was slow and regular.

A dark spinal column dripped from the park lamp above him. Was that even *possible?*

If the Horselord marked Victor's approach, he gave no sign. As the bow rose in Brum's hand, poised against the night, Victor could see the branded body of the violin: "Warranted 40% genuwine Havana tobacco." A sticker read "Product of Dodoville."

Brum struck the low string. The catgut creaked and moaned. Like a dance partner, the current caught up the sound and waltzed it downstream. The bow flashed again; Brum struck the high string. It whimpered and screeched. The river snatched the note like royal decree and rode it hard from Dodoville's seaward shore toward the ocean. The bow flashed as it cut across strings, a blur of hand working a war of slashes and thrusts, tracing a history carved into the city's rotwood flesh: the aluminum worker scalded to death at his press station, the black marketeer fed to eels amid cheers on the stage of the Mountebank Theater,

184

the hermit who starved through bitter winters upon barren crags. Victor heard them all in the song that sprang from Brum's hand.

Weird and lively now, the melody soldiered on in a bandy-measured march, in mountain shadow shuddering as glittering-insane gouts of terror and love were hurled from its fiery maw. It sang a celebratory dirge, a mournful triumph, a rage against fate, and an embrace of ruin. Fevered dreams of beautifying illness, an encore an overture, a sound, a sonnet, a hell-born roar.

All this Brum summoned and cast off into the river. Into time, into stillness and death. Played upon a moldy box with a crooked stick unfit to stir soup.

Around them, the strewn and broken bodies listened with dead ears. Had their life not been torn out through newly-cut orifices, the faces would have worn no less surprise to confront such depth of soul in this sordid little park on the city outskirts.

"We have to finish this," spoke the Violet Storm into one of the lulls, cracking his knuckles inside a yellow glove.

A wrathful moon, pocked and scarred from the predation of stars and comets, hurled down a spear of light from its perch in heaven. Like a stone, the warhead skipped across the river's limpid stream to shatter its glow harmlessly upon the knight's broad chest. Brum resumed his elegy upon the violin, his bow countering the moon strike-for-strike as if this struggle between him *and it* were the more immediate danger. In fury, he played. Against the cold illumination of the cosmos, against karma, against remiss springs that brought his soul no renewal, against the annual club fees that did renew but without his confirmation.

Victor hated to get pushy during Brum's bout of introspection. Still, he sighed loudly and pretended to glance at the watch he wasn't wearing.

If anything, the enormous man played even slower, more mournfully, like he was trying to smash you over the head with his fucking sadness.

"I'll come back next week," Victor said sarcastically, his patience running thin.

The fiddle paused. Brum spoke softly into the silence.

"A few weeks ago, they told me my mother had died. Said I should go home and put affairs in order." He raised the bow again as if to play, but let it fall soundlessly at his side. "I . . . don't keep 'affairs.' When I come, the neighbor woman had the body laid out on the bed in the upper room. Exactly where I left her when I run away as a boy. Every stick of furniture the same, I saw. The wallpaper. I'd left all this then to leave it. So what was I doing here now?"

Brum looked between the bow and violin as if he'd never seen either before.

"I decided to burn the house down, figured that'd be the handiest way. Take care there are no loose ends. Before I dropped the torch, I saw a bundle of letters by the bedside. Thought they might be key to finding the stash mother hid during the gang wars, so I gave 'em a look. No luck. Letters I had written. To a girlfriend, long ago. The day I left home, of course, I didn't tell her goodbye. The girl got angry and mailed back all she had of me. Mother kept 'em all those years."

He set the fiddle beneath his chin again and adjusted one of the tuning keys. He sounded a chord. Worse. Much worse. The notes flat and whimpering, he forced his way through some old children's melody.

"I read the letters. Skimmed. Mostly to see how one fills so much paper. Made no damn sense at all, those words. Love anger or lust, it all sounded the same to me. But what struck me was."

He played now as if creating beauty were a moral failing, as if in defiance of his hand the strings confessed his flaws. A man for whom brutality was the only virtue.

Suddenly he stopped.

"I sounded like anyone else. That chatter people fill their lives with. Look at me, who am I, what'm I about. My life, too, once made of words. Today I am Brum. Brum is what Brum does. To tell what's inside here," he touched his chest, the soft spot above the armpit, "I'd have to show you. There is nothing to tell. I am Brum, that is all."

Somewhere behind them, Mt. Myrtle grumbled listlessly, repressing her deathly inclination for another hour. The heat of the day had broken, and condensation wept down the stones of the river wall, over dark mosses and spray-painted vulgarities, evoking a rich odor from the black muck below.

"Look around you, Onion, the landscape." His finger pointed as he named them. "Willows. Water. Sky. If ever you

187

chose not to speak of these again, you would forget the words. You'd forget they have names."

He was silent a moment. His chin rose, his eyes gazing toward the moon.

"Today there are no names for the landscape of Brum."

Victor wondered if the knight knew how to hear his own violin, if he cared that it betrayed how even Brum the Destroyer could not unwrite the humanity in his genes. Victor imagined a prisoner in solitary confinement, looking through the arrow slit in the wall that let in the only air, waiting for the moon to pass so he could look up and try to find his living self on its ancient barren face.

"Go away, Onion. Take your camera. You have carried the day, but for you, I have only silence."

The device hidden on Victor's jumpsuit was in fact recording. The little red light was on.

The two men exchanged a brief glance of understanding. As the knight's bare torso turned again toward the river, the regal lion tattooed across his shoulders seemed to shrink and cower.

Victor nodded and disappeared into the willows, his slippers squelching in the fresh gore as he left.

Surely, Dodoville had heard the last of Knight Commander Brum.

The Storm Cycle's single headlight cut through the fog on the mountain road. Disengaging the purple filter and the running lights, he wove in and out among the night smugglers—fast enough to make them feel suction in his wake.

Vroooom! What an awesome day! He'd had a car wreck, ziplined like a ninja into battle, jousted as a knight errant, meteored like a meteor, and acted kinda paternal as a father-confessor. By the time he got back to the *Spyhole*'s offices, his chief editor, Citroën von Chesterdrawer, would have a front page splash ready for the morning edition. *Violet Storm confronts Dodoville's most ancient enemy; defeats them across the arc of heaven like a modern-day god.*

More terse, though, probably.

Till now his vigilante exploits had met with mixed opinion, but tomorrow he would be Dodoville's hero. Because his battle against the Pestilence had been frickin' cool. And nothing tops cool.

Up ahead, he saw an unpaved offramp marked "No Trafficking Permitted." He took this exit, racing until the road dead-ended in a wall of collapsed rubble. At the last moment, he skidded out onto a spur. A motorized ramp accelerated the bike over a clay pit—where he executed a superman seat grab, even though no one was looking. He landed in a cement basin that opened into the old municipal drainage system.

189

Victor leaned low to clear the ceiling as the Storm Cycle entered the tunnel.

Experimental ambient music played on his helmet speakers as wall-lights ignited to guide him through the maze beneath the city. The pattern of colors, purple mixed with kelly green and lemon yellow, spiraled around him or lashed back and forth above. The Storm Tunnels, he called them. He sped up, making ever sharper and more dangerous turns, the walls seeming to narrow around him.

"Mori, come in."

A transparent image of the skiapod butler appeared on his helmet visor. Totally not in a dangerous way.

Caught mid-butle, Mori straightened and turned toward him. "Yes, Master Victor," he said solemnly.

"Pestilence neutralized. ETA three minutes. Prepare my car. I'm headed to the *Spyhole*."

The comm dropped as Victor upshifted for more VROOOOM.

On the final approach, an earth bridge carried the bike high above a magma runoff from the central vein below Mt. Myrtle. The heat was brutal: engines could give out quickly here. Human bodies too.

The chopper squeezed through a fissure in the rock wall. Blasts of icy air dimpled his riding leathers as he passed into the Storm Lair. The aggressive cooling system served as life support for the three-story corridor of surveillance equipment, satellite downlinks, matrix analysis cubes, and data platter arrays.

Mounted high on the ceiling and pulsing with a vascular lavender light was String-o, the digital heart of the Violet Storm operation. This was the Boswell Institute's breakthrough computational lattice-mesh, a semi-conscious engineering miracle that housed a duoverse processing core with twin onboard hexeracts to implement nine-dimensional quantum sorcery. Times two.

The chopper whispered to a halt on the receiving platform across from the machinist bay. The platform rotated for some reason.

Mori awaited him, bobbing slightly at the knee. Although this was resting state for a skiapod, the motion lent his appearance an overeager air.

Victor tossed Mori the key to the bike. From a proffered tray, he snatched the keys to the Duesey parked outside Davy Castle, ready to take him to the *Spyhole* building in center city. He strutted off to his wardrobe to pick out a change of clothes.

Mori bounded after him. "You've defeated them all, sir?" Undoubtedly tracking Victor's activity, he must have known the answer.

"No," Victor replied dryly. "I had to leave the wimpy one behind to chase down the ringleader."

He caught Mori glancing askew at the key in his hand. Constructing the Storm Cycle to Victor's fussy design specifications had made it somewhat impractical for a one-legged skiapod to valet.

"I wouldn't leave any loose ends, sir," Mori said politely.

191

"The Pestilence's remaining members will be advancing now on the mission's primary target."

Victor stopped. "The *primary* target?"

Mori looked embarrassed. "Or. One should be sure, in any case, sir."

Victor snagged a computer console and scanned the emergency dispatches around Dodoville. The sites of the Pestilence's offensives appeared on a city map, marked with miniature explosions. Blue red and yellow arrows also indicated movement of police, fire, and medical. It looked like a Jackson Pollock.

"A mad dash crisscrossing the city," he muttered. "Emergency personnel deployed everywhere. Creating disruptions."

"Yes, *crisscrossing*."

Victor stared at him mutely.

"Casting a *wide net*." The butler offered an encouraging smile. Victor wanted to slap it off.

"Remember, sir," Mori said patiently, "everywhere they went, the knights gave only haphazard attention to the police. Clearly, you were the one they wanted to engage."

"Of course. Cumin Media's intelligence network is larger and more sophisticated than the cops'."

Mori shook his head. "The CKE doesn't know you are Victor Cumin, sir. They only know you as the Violet Storm." Subtle emphasis on *violet*.

"Who can defeat any one of them in single combat."

"Perhaps, sir. But remember, the Church of the Knight Errant has thousands of members, many of which train secretly in equestrian arts. Today they sent only four."

Three of whom he had given a sound public beating. The work now was to ensure his people at the *Spyhole* presented the story correctly. He hacked into von Chesterdrawer's computer to see how the bald old fart was mangling this one.

"Four is a biblical number," he snarled, finally hearing Mori's comment.

The skiapod shrugged. "So is forty."

He was right. The four was important. But not for symbolic reasons.

"Logistics," Victor mumbled.

Mori giggled, bobbing more vigorously now.

Victor sighed. "They didn't send more marauders because they don't have enough equestrian armor. They need more spider-silk."

The console screen summoned an image of what looked like a mothballed factory in a wooded clearing. An animated neon purple webbing flashed across it.

"Once they acquire enough" Victor said, "they'll be unstoppable."

The skiapod clapped, his hands fluttering like little bird wings. "That does seem a concern, sir."

Victor scowled at his display of excitement.

"String-o!" he shouted.

The computer's translucent wiring flushed purple to indicate attention.

"Full CCTV sweep of Dodoville. Show me: Sir Bubo Skymole, Club Towers, and Ariadne's Arachnophilia Euphorium."

A jumbo holograph map of the city appeared on a table in front of him. The tower dominated the downtown in red. The 3D model was so detailed you could see a little Abhoc in handcuffs, still telling stories to bystanders while he waited for the police to load him into the van.

Deep in the forest, the spider den loomed in black. Bubo appeared on the edge of the wood in yellow. His vector graphic showed he was not moving.

"String-o, what is Sir Bubo doing?"

A live camera feed of the knight switched on. He was inside a mountain supply store, packing a body-length shoulder bag.

"Acquiring additional weaponry, a sewing kit, and salty snacks."

String-o's voice was unimaginably horrible, as if the words were spoken by a dying lamb, both forward and backward at once, also diagonally, inside out, underwater, and with a stutter, all rolled up in a ball and mixed with ground teeth and peanut butter.

It made Victor want to vomit out his eyeballs. Even Mori frowned a little.

"Can we do anything about that?"

"The voice?"

"No, the other soul-shredding sound horror!"

Mori shrugged. "I don't believe so, sir. That's the noise String-o projects from the six pocket dimensions posited by superstring theory."

"Why not put a filter on it?"

"Along which pocket dimension do you wish to install it?" Mori asked reasonably.

"Then how 'bout we just posit a different theory?"

Mori looked nervous. "That governs all time and space throughout the multiverse, you mean, sir?"

"Yeah."

He scratched his jaw thoughtfully. "Hum. I'll see what I come up with tonight," he said.

"String-o, if you have anything else to add, say it through interpretative dance."

The computer's mass of wiring shifted into some rather rude-looking emoji.

"Thanks, girl," Victor said, blowing it a kiss.

"Sir, I should warn you: the trade-off for making String-o's circuitry invulnerable to flooding, magma, and ESD is that it has almost no tolerance for being patronized."

"Mori, phone von Chesterdrawer." Victor snatched up his onion mask from where it hung on the monitor. "Tell him to not to wait for me to put the paper to bed tonight. Say I have to bully/blackmail some investors again."

"Very good, sir."

He turned, whispering. "Also, you know my unbreakable

quarterstaff? Brum broke it. Can you fabricate me something else?"

"Not without notice, sir," the butler replied cheerily.

"Mori—"

"Which is why I began this morning!" The way his face beamed struck Victor as mildly psychotic.

"Perfect. You got about ten minutes. That's about how long it'll take me to figure out how to take a leak in this getup."

"Oh peaches, sir! Of course, I thought of that. All you have to do is . . ."

"Ten minutes, Mori! Don't you ever take a breather?"

"Honestly, sir, I wouldn't know what to do if—"

"Finish my damn weapons! I probably have like fifty dudes to fight!"

The bathroom door slammed shut.

The skiapod hopped to work. But only barely enthusiastically.

•

In the distance, the dark shape of the Euphorium lay like a half-buried stone in an overgrown field.

Victor hid the Storm Cycle in the brush and made the final approach on foot, treading silently down an old cart path that cut through the tall grass. About him, the air teemed with tiny white puffs floating across his field of vision. Dandelion umbrellas. As the moon poked through the cloud cover, they exploded into pinpricks of white fire. How magical!

After a moment, he noticed the puffs were not the right shape. They were animal, not vegetable. Activating the magnifying scope on his digital eyepiece, he saw the legs held together in a tight bouquet, the fibrous hairs and the haunting arrays of eyes, and—was he imagining it?—the tiny glint of fangs. A flight of spider hatchlings was flurrying around him, ballooned on gossamer parachutes into the surrounding woods. Such a wealth of crafty hunters spawned here that most of their offspring had to trust themselves to the turbulent mountain winds for a chance at survival. They were carried across punishing Kolkhek heights or down into the river valley on the capricious furnace blasts of the volcano. Sometimes they even caught an updraft into the jet stream and ventured the wide world over.

Victor flung his arms open and let them scurry over him: the white and brown ones, black and speckled ones, meaty and leggy ones, deflecting off his body like driven snow.

The shriek a man makes at the sight of a spider is unlike the one he makes at his own reflection. For this terror is not of what is but what he has failed to become, what God in her wisdom or cruelty has declined to make him.

His late mother's voice echoed in his ears. Twenty years after Rochelle Cumin's death, Dodoville still remained under her influence. The *Spyhole* still bore her masthead, and even the Violet Storm, Victor suspected, somehow served as her agent.

It was true that as one of her last acts, Rochelle had helped install the Consortium, the gangland regime Victor now used all his skill and knowledge to undermine—but hadn't it always been her way: cast a web and later abandon it, use the strength she imbibed from her successes to lay a bigger trap for more powerful prey?

Beyond the clearing, Victor's eyepiece detected something moving through the undergrowth: agile as it was enormous, featherlight so the leaves hardly rustled in its wake.

He pressed on.

Ariadne's Arachnid Euphorium was a refurbished textile factory, one that had produced "medieval" Dodovillean tapestries in the late 1990s. After a mudslide buried much of it, a new main entrance had been punched into the upper story. Beside the door, a whimsical neon sign flashed "FLIES WELCOME." Below that, in hand-painted letters: "Business Hours 9am - 3pm."

No one had been euphoric enough to post the name of the enterprise anywhere.

Bubo's mare stood hitched to a post out front, grazing contently. Victor remembered from his surveillance report that her master had given her an off-putting name: Toad.

He examined the front door. Open. No sign of forced entry. He stepped inside.

In the dark, he found a gift shop. Adorable plush spiders. Decorative cobwebs. Postcards, silly string, bouncy rubber balls, T-shirts with four extra arms. A small library of coffee table books. A cellophane tube full of plastic bugs and worms. It all felt rather twee, even in the creepy neon glow of the window sign. Yoo-fucking-phoria.

Victor strode behind the counter and passed through the employees' entrance to the back rooms.

An aseptic fluorescent-lit hallway terminated in a steel door. Key card lock, biometric scanner, and some kind of elaborate puzzler. Weaver Hall, the sign offered. DANGEROUS: KEEP OUT. This warning appeared on overlapping stickers that covered the metal portal from floor to lintel. It was propped open with a piece of wood.

Slipping inside, he emerged on a catwalk suspended above the loomworks. Below, the room teemed with tens of thousands of tiny bodies darting around pinwheel warps in reducing concentric paths. A deft apparatus, called the nelly, picked up webs, untangled the fibers, and spooled them away. Another machine twisted strands together to make them thicker and stronger. On the level below, a battery of machines dyed the silk and wove it into bolts, which were stacked on palettes in the corner.

Square miles of material. Nobody supervising the work. The process seemed fully automated.

Victor had underestimated the scale of this operation. And its significance.

For two decades now, nearly every financial asset coming in and out of Dodoville had to pass through the hands of the Consortium. For that reason, no rival gang had managed to scrounge up significant opposition. But the production of a lightweight ballistics-resistant material could bring in an independent stream of funds from governments and private citizens across the globe. Any gang that controlled this factory would be able to offer the Consortium the first real challenge to its authority in a generation.

Should it fall into the hands of the CKE, Dodoville's future was lost. At least the Consortium wanted something to hold tyranny over! The Pestilence would pillage the city and raze its buildings to the ground. How many silk-armored horses would they need? With no more than four, they had overrun the police, then terrorized the shopping district, the suburbs, and the night entertainment center. With a hundred riders, not even an army could stop them.

At the far end of the catwalk, the knight known as Bubo Skymole stepped out of the shadows. He had a drumstick in his hand and was eating messily.

"I'd hoped to give you the slip, Onion," he said, wiping the animal grease from his chin. "Or should I say . . . the *dip*?"

"That doesn't even make any sense," said the computerized voice through Victor's mask.

"Twook-ker-dem-jeet!" Bubo growled. "I don't give a fuck."

Something about the Pestilence's quartermaster had changed. He still moved with that afternoon's awkwardness, but his bearing had soured, and he seemed disinclined to grant deference to anybody. Victor suspected he was about to confront the technician's true form.

"Didn't you like my party?" he said, his voice petulant. "I did so much planning to make you go home content. The finest knights of the realm delivered into your hands! The most conspicuous battle sites, so you'd gorge yourself on the media coverage you crave. And to top it off: I laid down a really bitchin' soundtrack for you to fight to, from a stereo system mounted on my *horse!* What more do ya want?"

Well, it'd definitely been a unique day, Victor thought. Engaging in deathly combat while a crowd swayed and sang "The Chain" had been the most surreal moment of his life. And he fought criminals in a onesie and slippers.

"I am the servant of Dodoville," the Violet Storm pronounced, "not publicity. And I shall not rest until you and your kind are driven from the city. Forever this time."

Bubo threw the half-eaten bone over the rail and watched it catch in the webs being woven by gorgeous orb spinners.

He shrugged. "That's a good line. But if I had you balled up and sobbing right now, what would you confess to? Just wanting to help people? I dunno, maybe. Maybe not!"

Something about the threatening note in Bubo's voice made Victor's endocrine system clear his thoughts and soothe his nerves. The tingle of tranquility spread like meltwater to his extremities.

"You'll have to defeat me to find out," he said serenely.

"Just a minute." He licked the grease from his fingers. "Before we get to the threat-making portion of the evening, I just want to thank you for making the resurgence of the

Horselords possible. We simply did not have the technology to accomplish it. Sure, we had jet engines and awesome weaponry. Our combat skills were whetted to a fine edge. But you just couldn't win our kind of war anymore. Once upon a time, they had to build walls to keep us out. Now walls were no longer necessary. We were forced to live among our enemies and work beside them. To our disgrace, we sent our children to school with their children. All hope seemed lost. But then you."

Bubo clasped his palms together in a gesture of gratitude and admiration.

"The unstoppable fighting force who cheated bullets and the blades of knives. Live electricity danced in his hands but did him no harm. But how? Must be the purple suit. Not just any purple, but the same color as the ash of Yterpokhok—the sacred mountain heathens call Myrtle. Somehow the volcano itself infused the fabric with its power."

The knight leaned nonchalantly on the railing, an oily satisfaction on his face.

"First we assumed some sort of plant fiber, a secret left over from the reign of Big Botany. Nope. Next—oh you'll get a laugh out of this—we thought it was wool. For months we *believed* someone was herding super sheep up on a mountain crag. Funny, right? Laugh. I have to. Then one day, I was watching that Superman movie where they hold up a ton weight with one of his hairs. I know it doesn't make any sense, but the moment I saw that, I knew the answer. Spiders! Steel-strength strands, just like the Man of Steel. After that, it was just a trip to the library. The lilaportia, the tiniest of the earth's web spinners, who lay their eggs exclusively in the hot ash of our sacred mountain. The problem is, even harvesting thousands of these little fuckers, we couldn't make more than a square centimeter a day. We were about to give up."

Bubo smiled. "Then we found out about this place. We were, how do you say? Euphoric."

"A pity you came so far for nothing," said Victor, his voice eerily calm. "You are no match in combat for me, Sir Skymole. And you are all alone!"

"Am I?" Bubo pulled a gladius from his belt. Sized for the small knight, the sword looked no bigger than a toy, and he made a show of pretending he didn't know which way was up. It slipped from his hands and fell from the catwalk, clattering loudly on the floor below.

"Aw, shucks. Now I'm defenseless." He giggled.

Victor heard something moving in the darkness above.

"Today the ride of the Pestilence had four legs," Bubo explained, "same as a horse. But horses are our people's past. Spiders are its future. Besides, did you think I meant to carry off an army's worth of silk on my own?"

Eight coils of silk rope unraveled as eight warriors descended soundlessly from the shadowy ceiling, a loose knot wrapped around one of their ankles. With a deft movement, they twisted and bent until they stood with a foot in a loop like a stirrup. All of them were women.

Victor rose his fists in a battle stance and surveyed his

opponents. They wore cloth armor with a kerchief over their mouths like bandits. Their hair hung straight and loose to their shoulders, all dyed to the same shade of blond, regardless of skin tone. Each wore a transparent eyepatch; it kept the dust out but let you see the raw wound beneath, where each woman had made the sacrifice of Odin for whatever power or wisdom they might purport to possess. Their iron skull helms had tiny heifer horns upon them.

"Perhaps you have heard of the Church's shieldmaidens? Probably not. For she whose virtue is greatest is spoken of the least. But like us knights, they know Dodoville is ripe to be bled. A hundred years in exile, our females have honed their skills up in the Kolkhek mountains where the tyranny of Dodoville could not corrupt them or their freeborn sons. Agile as an avalanche, they move among the most dangerous heights, snatching prey from the mouths of leopards, tearing birds out of the sky above terrifying drops. They are a match for you, Onion."

He smiled sweetly. "I know you like a challenge."

That's a lot of warrior ladies, Victor thought.

In each pair of hands, a different weapon. Meaning he'd need a different battle response to each, and all coming at him at once. Tonight would require a virtuoso performance on his part.

"Ladies, please," Victor said, "surely you have no truck with these jokers. They think King Arthur was Christ's middle name. I doubt warriors as clever as yourselves would buy into any of that?"

204

"Well, my shieldmaidens," cried Bubo, "What do you buy into? Inform our raisin-colored adversary!"

The women exchanged sidelong glances.

"Tell him your promise to Odin. Use your *voice!*"

Quietly at first, then as if emerging below from some secret cavern, a low roar boiled and bubbled around him. It was a cry of defiant agony, of someone trying to speak who could not. They tore the kerchiefs from their faces. Instead of words, dark fluid dribbled from their mouths. He could see now why they didn't speak: their lips were sewn shut!

"This is a ritual the Church's shieldmaidens elect to undergo before battle. It signifies that in war, talk is cheap, that action is paramount."

"Then why are you so chatty?" Victor quipped.

Fanatics, he thought. He didn't like the mechanical determination in their eyes . . . Eye. If he could run a finger across their minds, he was sure it would squeak, they had been washed so clean.

"I suppose they don't confess," Victor mused.

"No," replied Bubo. "And Horsefolk women don't cry. So you are going to need to invent some new tactics, Onion. Some new method to bully the free people of the Kolkhek mountains!"

Freedom to continue a war that ended in the nineteenth century. One of the most bizarre definitions of that word Victor had heard yet.

Well, nothing to do for it, he guessed. He would have to fight them over this pit of arachnid horrors with the fate of Dodoville on the line. At least he had Mori's new weapon for the fight. If only the skiapod had had a moment to ·explain its special features.

He snatched up the short battle rod he wore on his belt and hit the activation button. He heard a low hum as it came online, then watched as it telescoped apart. Compartments opened, components extended, attachments locked into place. Balloons inflated.

Victor stared at the martial absurdity in his hand. It looked like a swiss army knife of clown tricks used to entertain at children's parties.

Well, he thought, *at least nobody will die bored today!*

•

High in Weaver Hall, a partition opened in the wall, and Ariadne stepped out onto her secret surveillance station. Her feet tread noiselessly on the metal grating. Not even light and shadow bent around her.

At a glance, she sized up the situation: ten invaders in her domain. Two males on the catwalk, puffing their feathers. Eight females hanging close to the ceiling—they seemed to believe they were hiding!

Down in the loomworks, hundreds of thousands of tiny eyes, paired to hundreds of thousands of hard-working legs, glanced to Ariadne for instruction. She spoke at a frequency beyond the threshold of human hearing, which only the fine hairs upon the tiny bodies could detect and interpret. *Protect the fabric, my daughters. Protect the work.*

All at once, spinners, weavers, and spoolers abandoned their posts and assumed defensive footing. In perfect readiness to fight, to die if necessary.

It wouldn't be. Mostly Ariadne wanted to keep them out of the way.

The cheek of these people, she thought, *coming to my den to fight. As if Dodoville's future was theirs to decide!*

The city had just shy of a million human inhabitants. Every ten to twenty years, some upheaval of their own making overturned everything, burying their labors, erasing the lessons of their sweat and sorrow. Damning them to start over yet again.

Here in the Euphorium, two million citizens—industrious, dexterous, dutiful, indefatigable—lived and worked toward a tomorrow of their own design, handing down skills across eons in an unbroken chain, mother to daughter. Everyone here had thousands of mothers.

This enclave of spiders had arrived in the Kolkheks before there was a Sporqia or a Dodoville, before hermits came to the mountains to pray, or horseback marauders to torment them.

Ah, so that's the Purple Onion, come dressed in our glory, Ariadne observed. *I see he favors the mother. If not for her warm blood, she might have made a queen among spiders. For her sake, I choose him now for our champion. He's impulsive and foolhardy, but under the guidance of the skiapod, a force to be reckoned with. I see the old general has armed him*

207

with the taqarhiza, *the weapon with which his beleaguered people turned back Alexander of Macedon in the Indus Valley. It will please me to see it do good service in battle again.*

Though the Onion had not yet noticed his opponents in the rafters, his body instinctively squared itself toward each combatant in turn, assuming a posture of confidence and strength. *His instincts are pure, I'll grant him that.*

Ariadne examined the shieldmaidens next. They were strong and limber, but where she ought to have sensed apprehension, she found nothing: parts of their survival instinct had simply been unwritten.

Unfortunate. When a spider fights, she can afford to cast away fear, trusting her strength and cunning to testify to her worth. Should she fall, she knows her sisters will cultivate her daughters in her stead, and her mind and work will survive in them. Not so for the human. Its body is weak, its mind riddled with error, and when it dies, its existence is lost forever. For that reason, it must rely on fear as its ally.

Yet take heart, shieldmaidens, Ariadne thought, *for today the rewards for valor shall be great. Your captors have torn something out of you—but impress me, and the Order of Araneae will make this void a keyhole, which we will use to unlock your true potential.*

The little knight gave the signal, and together the maidens spun down on their silk ropes. They descended artlessly, like wrecking balls. But admirable enough for mammalian bodies, she supposed.

Eight warriors they were. Needle and thread had sealed their voice, so let their weapons name them! Hand-axe, Sword, Pike, Morning Star, Poniards, Bullwhip, Mace, and ah, the Onion's beloved Quarterstaff!

Now they were just posturing at each other! *Why are they wasting time?* fumed Ariadne. *As if this isn't a place of work!* She found human mouth-noise theater unbearable.

"Shall we to the slaughtering now?" she thought, mimicking their hairless ape voices. *"Yes, I am much for the fighting of you! Wait, my shoeknot is unstickied!"*

The loom spiders, too, waited and watched.

As two human eyes make reason of three spatial dimensions, a spider's eight comprehend all nine, fusing together not only height and depth, but darkness and light, effect and cause, future and past.

With one foot, each maiden wrapped a silk stirrup around the other leg, granting her purchase to jump. From line to line the maidens flew, brandishing steel and strong ash, striking the air as they circled.

In the center of the storm stood the Onion, an eye of calm at the heart of the cyclone.

He waited. Surrounded and outnumbered was his element, after all. *Make the first mistake,* his bearing dared them. The maidens, not unlike the goat-stalking leopards of the Kolkheks, were solitary hunters, accustomed to fighting at dangerous elevations—but not together. If the Onion could disrupt their rhythms, their war dance would devolve into a stammering two-step. He could knot their limbs and bind them in defeat.

A first attack! Pike tested him with a thrust and a grunt. The point fell centimeters short of his mask. The Onion did not flinch, did not bat it away. Control, conservation—he'd need them to carry the day against these odds.

The shieldmaidens continued to swirl, leaping from rope to rope. Their weapons cut the air, hoping to draw a blow and leave an opening for another sister to exploit. But the Onion kept his defenses up and waited.

As Sword leaped past him, he gazed into her empty eye socket, lurid and defiant behind its dust shield. In turn, her one good eye saw a gold flash in both his pupils, bright enough to plant a seed of doubt in her mind whether her opponent was a man at all.

Suddenly, a war cry. The ululation, barred at the lips, echoed inside the mouth like a gagged scream.

Hand-axe was swinging boots first into the Onion. He twisted away and slapped her shoulders with the *taqarhiza* as she passed. She backflipped from the rope and landed facing him on the catwalk, bringing her axe down on his head with wide-eyed (singular) fury. He parried crosswise and kicked. She hopped away to evade while Sword launched herself into the gap. A fruitless exchange between her and the Onion blocked the follow-up from Hand-axe, who smashed the handrail of the catwalk in frustration.

The shieldmaidens simply did not have enough room. The catwalk was too narrow, it was too difficult to coordinate an attack without slashing and battering each other.

Bubo Skymole scurried up a ladder. From this vantage, he began to bark orders in the Horsefolk Old Tongue, to give shape to the maidens aimless assault.

Mostly he's up there to keep his freckled face from getting bashed open, thought Ariadne.

Quarterstaff signaled Bullwhip and Poniards. On her mark, these nimblest three leaped together. One after the other, they swung into the space where the Onion stood. He parried awkwardly, the trailing tethers of his weapon's *jorlyghul* snaking on the catwalk and confounding his movement.

The exchange left him contorted and off balance, but the Onion recovered before Hand-axe could push to the front.

Ariadne cackled. *The Purple Onion has never even seen the* taqarhiza *in battle before*! she realized. *He's no more competent with it than the shieldmaidens in coordinating their attacks. Oh, the fools in my house!*

It would be a race then. Who would figure it out first?

To tell the truth, Morning Star knew no better than the Onion how to wield her weapon—surely, she had never hunted hawks with this ridiculous thing! (It was not a spiked flail but the mace-and-chain that belongs more to modern imagination than to history.) Bubo's fantasy had been for each maiden to wield a different weapon. Offered first pick, she made this absurd choice in hopes he would abandon the idea. Instead, he had cackled in glee at her decision.

Anyway, she was willing to helicopter it over her head for show, but she had no intention of taking a spiked ball to face when it bounced off the Onion's ugly stick. She landed on the catwalk beside him and hip-checked him to the ground.

He kipped up and drove her back with a thrust.

The bullwhip cracked loudly and wrapped itself around the shaft of the *taqarhiza*. The Onion yanked its wielder forward as he parried a slice from Sword. As their eye(s) met once again, Sword winked and blew him a kiss with her sewn lips.

Gruesome! She seemed pretty pleased with her joke.

The Onion swept the legs out from under Bullwhip, who fell back onto the catwalk. She landed hard, driving the air from her lungs. Her nostrils flared as she tried to recover quickly.

Noticing how the Onion turned whenever one of the maidens landed on the catwalk, Mace threw a fire extinguisher behind him as Poniards attacked from the front. He parried Poniards neatly and struck her shoulder, but ignored the loud crash to steady his weapon at Sword, deterring a slash at his flank. The extinguisher rolled over the edge and fell below.

Ariadne rolled her eyes. *Bah! Mace is my least favorite of them for sure*, she thought.

With strength and precision, Sword sparred with the Onion, but her weapon was too heavy to match speed with the lightweight but sturdy *taqarhiza*. Fortunately, he was having a hard time not tripping on the *jorlyghul,* the twin tethers that trailed from the butt of the shaft and ended in air sacks that lay deflated on the catwalk.

You idiot! thought Ariadne. *You are holding the classic skiapod weapon. Fight like a skiapod!*

When mastered, the *taqarhiza* was like a conductor's baton directing the enemy to their own destruction. It worked particularly well while facing hopeless odds. But wielded by the uninitiated, it was about as useful as a pool noodle.

Hand-axe, her balance as keen as her blade's edge, landed upon one of the catwalk handrails. She leaped over the flailing *jorlyghul* in a double somersault and landed in a split across the railings, bringing her weapon down viciously at the Onion's head. The blade fell about a centimeter short. The Onion winked playfully at her.

If battle is your profession, thought Ariadne, *always have as many eyes as possible. It doesn't take Sun Tzu to know that!*

Mace continued to pick her way around the outside, looking for an opening. A few of her sisters were faster, the rest had weapons with longer reach. It was up to her then to find the advantages the others were too busy to see. Perhaps she could sabotage the catwalk he stood on, or use the colossal loom mechanisms against him? Or maybe there was a way to unleash the fury of the spiders . . .

If that one doesn't do something soon, thought Ariadne, *I'll take care of her myself!*

The Purple Onion's usual tactic was to break down his opponent physically until he had defeated them mentally. But that approach was too limited against eight ferocious warriors who gave him little chance to catch his breath.

Seven and a quarter, adjusting for Mace, Ariadne thought.

With his attention divided between Quarterstaff and Pike, Sword spotted an opportunity. Silent as a raptor on wing, her saber curved and sharp as a talon, she floated in behind to deliver a decapitation blow at the base of the Onion's skull.

At the last moment, he grappled Pike and threw her over his shoulders at Sword, who barely avoided cutting her sister in two!

That Onion had more eyes in his head than a potato.

The two maidens collided midair, dropping their weapons on the catwalk as they fell into the loomworks below. Spiders swarmed to protect the silk.

Before their sisters could vanish into the flurry of tiny bodies, Mace and Morning Star dropped down to rescue them from the skeeving-out of a lifetime. As the four women climbed hand-over-hand back up the ropes, spiders slid off their bodies in sheets.

Even with half his opponents now diverted, the Onion experienced no let up in the fighting. The remaining warriors, having less difficulty keeping out of each other's way, laid into him more fiercely than before. Not only was he warding off blows on all sides, he had to untangle himself periodically from the *jorlyghul!*

The taqarhiza *is a sacred weapon,* Ariadne thought. *That radioactive brussel sprout is going to fight with it correctly if he likes it or not!*

Ariadne opened her mouth and called inaudibly into the darkness. A gray spider dropped from the ceiling and landed on the catwalk where the Onion stood. Speedily, it climbed up and around the inside of his ankle and disappeared inside the purple slipper.

A howl rent the air inside Weaver Hall. The Onion collapsed to one knee. A torrent of swear words so vile followed, it almost made Ariadne blush. He cursed everything the sunlight touched, and he wished a plague of thorny horrors up every orifice it did not.

In agony, the Onion picked up the sword upon the catwalk. He seemed to consider lobbing the foot off.

Instead, he leaned on the *taqarhiza* and pulled himself back up. The injured limb would carry no weight. Still, he steadied himself and raised the weapon once more, inviting his adversaries to try him as he hopped and bobbed on his good leg.

You are welcome, thought Ariadne.

Along the shaft of the *taqarhiza*, an array of running lights came on one by one until the instrument hummed in his hands. The leather spheres at the end of the *jorlyghul* drew air as he bounced in place, and the bobbing action kept them floating on their tethers behind him. With the weapon leveled at Quarterstaff, the trailing *jorlyghul* blocked the approach of Bullwhip and Hand-axe on his four and eight o'clock. These two maidens circled counterclockwise, but spheres followed, now occluding his six and three. When the maidens batted them aside, the tethers went rigid and snapped back, again occluding their approach with the spheres.

The Onion swung the staff portion to beat back Quarterstaff. The tethers went limp, the stoma opening and deflating the spheres. Bullwhip and Hand-axe rushed in at the opportunity. As the Onion pivoted, the tethers whipped back, the slack spheres smacking them, administering a mild electric shock for good measure.

Poniards watched the Onion bob at the knee as if he had to pee really badly. Even with the spheres obstructing her approach, the injury to his foot ought to slow him enough that she could sneak in an attack with her small knives. She waited until he swung with the weapon, and allowed the spheres to pass before insinuating herself behind him for a strike. The two tethers, however, rotated around the axis of the shaft, carrying the forward momentum of the spheres back toward her. The deflated leather caught her under the chin with an uppercut.

Unfair! The next time a sphere passed, she double-stabbed it purely in protest. Both blades stuck inside, but the sphere didn't deflate. Like a flat-resistant tire!

Just to rub it in, the next time the Onion parried Quarterstaff, the *jorlyghul* struck Poniards across the mouth with the handle of her own weapon. It knocked a tooth loose, which she couldn't spit out, on account of her mouth being sewn shut. She wedged the bloody thing under her gums like a wad of tobacco and hoped she wouldn't choke as she carried on.

Without her poniards, Poniards became Kung Fu. Which was fine with her. The little daggers had no business in a melee, she thought. Besides, she should have been fucking Mace.

Pike, who was actually fucking Mace, had climbed out of the factory pit and recovered her weapon. She leaped from rail to

216

rail, trying to sneak up behind the Onion and make the *jorlyghul* knot around her polearm so her lover could attack from his flank.

Perhaps hunting in the mountains sounds like it promises a lot of personal freedom, but the Church of the Knight Errant, like many cults, exerted stifling sexual control over its members. A maiden had a curfew, and a chaperon checked her bed for occupancy (single) every evening and every morning. The chaperons were ill-tempered men carrying rather un-medieval sidearms. Ostensibly, they were also the maidens' trainers, despite never doing any of that cliff-leaping bullshit themselves, no way. Eating food the shieldmaiden hunted helped ensure she kept busy with her virtue-building mountaineering. Which was a kind of training, if you thought about it.

Amorous rendezvous were hard to arrange for Pike and Mace since they starved if they didn't hunt. But if they hunted together and split the spoils, some shooty bastard was gonna be like, Where's the other half of this hawk?

Anyways, now that the Onion had a good bobbing rhythm, the *jorlyghul* were everywhere inconvenient, pushing Pike back as if they had a mind of their own. Nevertheless, Ariadne noticed Pike was really good at leaping on handrails, which was a nice trick in armor.

Nobody leaped rope-to-rope as strongly as Mace, but from the way she held her weapon, anyone could tell she was no more dangerous in a fight with it than an ornery drunk. The rumor going 'round the CKE's monthly potluck was she was getting by on her looks. The truth was, Mace had been trying to fail out of the program for years now, but it's difficult to leave the shieldmaidens alive. Besides, her guardian had taken a shine to her and resented the idea of letting her go. She was hoping years of exposure to the harsh mountain climate would erode her value for him, but what retirement might entail frightened her as much as anything. In the meantime, she was just trying to get by.

Falcon eggs were delicious though.

While down among the factory machinery, Sword had grabbed a dangerous-looking metal spindle off one of the looms. To create an opportunity to reclaim her weapon, she threw it at the Onion. He screamed as it jabbed him in the ribs, but the sharp edge failed to pierce the silk armor. The projectile had nearly taken off the nose of Hand-Axe, however, who tried to make an "eat me" gesture at Sword, but again, her mouth was stitched shut.

Never let a cult sew up your orifices! thought Ariadne. *The government should put that on every lunchbox.*

The Onion recovered fast enough to land a solid blow to Hand-axe's hip, but expecting it to taze her as his quarterstaff did, he was lazy with the follow-up. Hand-axe countered with a solid punch to the ribs—right where the spindle hit him. Ow! Instinctively, she then tried to tear out his cheek with her teeth, but naturally, this too accomplished nothing.

Habits are hard to break, especially if you rely on instinct.

Pike always kept a few throwing stars on her belt for when

she'd been having a particularly long day and those mountain birds just kept circling up in the sky like she had nothing better to do. When the Onion had knocked Hand-axe to the ground, Pike saw a chance to hurl one at his face. It deflected off his mask and impaled itself in an extremely old orb weaver. She had been a mother or big sister for generations of spiders who manufactured bullet-proof lace underwear for the sexy and sexually-daring members of Her Majesty's Secret Service. Panties and brassieres are among the more difficult attire to make because the articles had to guarantee protection from a 55mm projectile while still serving up espionage couture and Bond girl realness.

Anyways, the Euphorium's entire lingerie department gathered round to pay the respects due to their fallen matriarch and mentor. Which may or may not have involved eating her. Who are you to judge?

While Mace's sisters tried to find some ingress against the Onion's now fully-functional weapon, she swung around the perimeter, doing God only knew what. To Ariadne, it looked like she was striking poses with her mace and performing unnecessary acrobatics on her silks, which nobody at all was watching.

Every chain has a weakest link, Ariadne thought, as she cut loose one of the sandbags near the ceiling. It knocked Mace square between the shoulders, hurling her face-first into a support beam, which split open the skin above her eye. As Mace came crashing down onto a pile of silk bolts, Ariadne saw her body assume an elegant free-fall pose, the kind that might be used as a silhouette in an art print or something.

Truly, all show and no substance.

A black weaver crawled over and sewed closed the wound on Mace's brow. Even though spiders are cold-blooded invertebrates, that's no reason they should be uncharitable.

Quarterstaff, Poniards, and Morning Star saw a new opportunity and attacked together. The Onion swung and held off Quarterstaff. He then hopped twice and reached back to parry Sword. The air sacks inflated behind him and caught Poniards (a.k.a. Kung Fu) like a lead balloon on the backswing. She reeled sharply and butted heads with Morning Star, who executed a little pirouette as she collapsed in a heap.

Morning Star lay on the catwalk, her legs dangling over the side. She was in a good position to swing her spiky ball up over her head and smash the Onion in the groin, something he seemed more aware of than her. More out of panic than malice, he thrust sharply downward with the *taqarhiza*. Its spearhead might have pierced her throat, if not for a company of weavers who had tied her ankles to a winch in the loom machinery. A harness of webbing tugged her sharply and winded her out of harm's way.

Seeing Morning Star laid out flat, a team of packaging spiders mistook her for product. Once they had bound her tightly, a crane loaded her on the forklift, which stacked her upright with the bolts of silk in the corner.

The Old Tongue of the Horselords in which Bubo barked

orders to the maidens was actually modern Danish. The Dodovillean immigrant who taught it to the CKE claimed it was their ancient language in hopes of getting them to purchase his hand-cooped bespoke barrels for their monthly keggers. But Bubo spoke it so badly, you might call it its own dialect.

Beaten to the ground and run over by Bullwhip, Hand-axe pulled herself to her feet, lowered her head, and charged back into the fray. Since finesse was proving useless in this fight, she was gonna try some old-fashioned get-the-fuck-out-of-my-way.

Kung Fu had finally worked back up to her hands and knees after her head collision with Morning Star. Her movement was wonky and she looked like she was trying to retch. *Gods help her if she has a concussion!* thought Ariadne. *Her mouth is too sewn shut to vomit!* She signaled her teamster spiders to swarm and haul her out of there immediately.

The Onion realized the air sacks at the end of the *jarlyghul* deflated automatically if he swung the *taqarhiza* in a wide arc, allowing him to fight freely. Operation of the weapon was proving fairly intuitive. Even up to his eyeballs in shieldmaidens, he spared a thought to marvel at Mori's design.

That small distraction cost him getting rammed in the ass with a pair of heifer horns.

Pike had a husband plus two children from a previous marriage. She found the term "shieldmaiden" condescending, but you just have to put up with shit like that if you want to be part of a cult, she felt.

A large gray ebo, which is a kind of crab spider, ventured into

Weaver Hall. As her species did not build webs, she was not a loom worker. She had only come to visit a friend when she saw all the fracas. It was too much sensory input, especially for someone with so many eyes! Feeling overwhelmed, she crawled out on Bubo's shoulder and bit his left ear. The knight smashed at her with a fist, which was a bad idea, because many spiders move faster than you'd think, and Bubo gave himself a pretty good whack where he'd just been injured.

The *taqarhiza* was basically a big titanium rod with a pair of balls attached. Mortal combat doesn't leave a lot of time for dick jokes, but damn! Damn is all I can say.

Quarterstaff stepped away from a blow to tease the Onion off balance. On the backpedal, she collided with the maiden behind her. The hand-axe flew from Hand Axe's hand and fell into the looms below. As the sharp edge struck a piece of cloth being woven on the woof, the blade merely bounced off the stretched fibers. Now that's strong!

Ker-rack!

Devastating blow! Maybe Onion hadn't mastered control the *jorlyghul* as well as he thought. The pommel of a poniard, still embedded in the leather sphere, cracked brutally against Bullwhip's shin and she collapsed on the catwalk. Pike dragged her out of the fight and examined the injury. Definitely a break. She snapped her pike in two and fashioned a splint for her warrior-sister.

Hand-axe swung down to the factory floor to recover her weapon. When she picked it up, the handle was covered in goo.

Some asshole spiders had shit their silk all over it! Well, no matter. Now she could cut his face off without losing her weapon again. Only . . . They had webbed the goddamn thing to the loom as well! She yanked and stretched, but no luck. She got a running start and jumped, but the silk bonds held. Frustrated, she tried to hack the web with the axe blade, but of course it wouldn't cut. All she accomplished was getting her arm enmeshed in the web too. Fuck!

Well, just because she was tied up didn't mean she couldn't smash at the loom with the axe head until she collapsed from exhaustion.

With most of the shieldmaidens neutralized, Quarterstaff was coming into her own. She was the tallest and leanest, also the oldest and the coolest under pressure. No longer facing overwhelming odds, the *taqarhiza* was proving less an advantage, the *jorlyghul* mostly just demanding extra precision from the Onion's movement. If she held his attention, hopefully an opportunity would open for Sword. Or bare-handed Pike could hit him with a flying tackle. The leadership at the CKE had been giving those two hell lately, so it would lift her spirits to help one of them score this victory.

As the battle's momentum shifted, Bubo's instructions became louder, more forceful, and almost exclusively directed at the one he called Jorza, which was not Danish but actual Old Horsefolk for darling or sweetheart, as every Dodovillean child knew from the school rhyme:

H'besh valekh, jorza nvru
zoldri na atba korbharul

Come swift, my *jorza*
Father's mare is about to foal

Even someone who had never attended a Dodoville school could see that Jorza was Quarterstaff, the only one to whom Bubo was paying attention.

Although no equal with that weapon to the Onion (who was approaching transcendence), she was holding her own. His M.O. was rarely to overpower but to make his opponent aware, volley by volley, that she faced a superior opponent. But Quarterstaff, incapable of discouragement, continued to try to draw him off and leave an opening for her comrades.

In response, the Onion seemed to be trying to test her, push her past her limits as a warrior.

Or maybe it was just hard to find a good sparring partner in the long stick these days.

Sword, a woman born Jordan Bosch, found it irritating that Bubo was speech-fucking Quarterstaff with a name that was practically hers. Out of the half dozen romantic poems about pregnant mares bleeding to death, Bubo had to borrow *that* name to sleaze on that ten-foot ninja lemur. Because of course, the knight had to drive it home how it was precisely *not* her he was cooing his martial nothings to.

When she was a girl, Sword's mother told her when she

joined a cult, the first thing was to learn how to take pleasure in the emotional abuse, because otherwise, she'd never find happiness. Her mother, the trophy wife of an odious businessman, had pushed her daughter toward cultism, since it was practically identical to her own life except without having to host elaborate dinner parties, which she considered the bane of her existence.

But what really ground her gears was that Quarterstaff, this so-called Jorza, would almost certainly lose a fight between the two of them, sword versus quarterstaff. Too bad Sword was only a deadly efficient and intuitive fighter, not some sky-high freak of nature with improbable, hypnotic-to-watch movements. Because if anyone here deserved a battle clinic on obsolete melee tactics from a grandmaster in spandex, it was Sword.

All of sudden, Sword realized that she hated horses and self-mutilation, and she hated charismatic cult leaders with wretched tasted in dance music. As for half-starving to death on a mountaintop while she trained in medieval weaponry—well, that was sorta cool, but what she really wanted was to run a little dry cleaners in town. For some reason she liked the chemical smells, and she could spend all day replacing coat zippers by hand. Not that she knew much about sewing (except the whip stitch she used on her mouth), but it had to be fucking easier than stabbing birds out of the goddamn sky for lunch.

So that's what she was going to do.

Her first step in opening a small business:

Striking a Poseidon pose, she crow-hopped and hurled her sword at Sir Bubo's heart.

The blade didn't cover even half the distance, since not even in a story this insane did the scimitar make a good javelin. The knight was too confused to even flinch.

Whether this had been a real assassination attempt or just a gesture of defiance, Sword-less stormed out of Weaver Hall in tears.

Pike, now Pike-less, foresaw no future where she first defeated the Onion with her fingernails then hauled off a half ton of silk on her shoulders. She ran after her warrior-sister into the hallway to comfort her.

Ariadne closed her eyes and imagined a crying jag between two armored women with their mouths sewed shut.

Her eyes instantly reopened. Not today, Satan, no way.

She instructed her servants to go check on the maidens and make sure they didn't steal more than one plush toy each from the gift shop.

Klop klop klop. Down on the floor, Hand-axe continued banging at the loom supports. Like trying to chop through an oak trunk with a really sharp spoon.

Only the Purple Onion and Quarterstaff remained. They exchanged blows, advancing and retreating, jumping ducking and rolling. The weapons crashed together, an elegant kiss of titanium on strong ash. Considering the duration of the battle, the spins and flourishes seemed extraneous and wasteful. No longer a struggle but a dance, the display of technique and stamina was pushing toward no resolution.

Bubo hopped up and down on the ladder, shouting with more bluster than sense, smashing the rails with a gauntlet to make as much noise as possible.

Ariadne sighed. This was entertaining, but she had a production schedule to keep. Time to choose: one to bind, one to set free.

The quality of the Onion's training was superior, but the maiden had fiercer determination and nothing left to lose. Each could prove an asset in their own way.

On the other hand, the Onion was a paying customer, the maiden was trying to steal a couple years' worth of product.

Ariadne had made her decision.

The banging on the factory floor continued.

•

"Enough!" a feminine voice cried.

Victor stopped fighting. Together with Bubo and 'Jorza,' he looked toward the rafters. No one was there.

Slowly, a purple and turquoise spider the size of a basketball descended on an invisible cable. The spines on her body looked meticulously brushed, and the eight orbs of her eyes blinked in a wave, from left-to-right then right-to-left.

Could this be who had spoken?

"I am Lady Ariadne," said the spider, "First of the Arachnids.

And you are trespassing in my domain! No work of the loom shall be removed from these premises without my permission, not on this day or any other! Shieldmaiden, submit!"

Jorza glanced over her shoulder to Bubo, who gestured: cut that hideous thing's head off.

She pulled a dagger from her boot and marched toward Ariadne. As she shouldered past Victor on the catwalk, she cast him a dead look with her one good eye. The hatred in the glance startled him so much, it didn't even occur to him to bar her way.

Suspended from the ceiling, the spider met Jorza face-to-face. The two exchanged a look that seemed to span oceans and centuries. The maiden held the flat of the dagger against her thigh.

Without further advisement, she knelt on the catwalk, bowed her head, and held out the dagger handle first toward Ariadne.

"Get up!" shouted Bubo, switching to passable English.

"Maiden," spoke Ariadne, "in lieu of punishment for your crimes today, you may pledge yourself in lifelong service to the Order of Araneae. In exchange, I will null and void your prior obligations and allegiances, severing all ties, by law or blood, vow or honor. Do you consent?"

"You have no authority to do so!" screamed Bubo as he descended his ladder. "The oath she swore is to the Lord God J. Harthur Christos himself!"

The room shook with the arachnid's voice.

"To whom do you speak, man-thing? For three millennia, I have stood before gods and bent them to my will! The Vulkan of this realm I hold in fief! Even the Mistress of Battles herself pays tithe to me. And you? Do you dare to charlatan fear in my house with your puny church? Favor your tongue and be silent!"

Bubo tilted his head. "Wait, you are *that* Ariadne?"

"Well, I'm not Ariadne Grande," she muttered. "Maiden, that faker has no power here. Do you consent then to my offer? Do you free yourself forever from his Church and swear yourself to me?"

Jorza raised her head and met Ariadne's eyes, forcing out two words through the blood congealed upon her sewn lips: I do.

A large gray spider landed heavily on the dagger, knocking it from her hands. Then it leaped and hugged her face, where it sprayed a dark liquid at her eyes and nose. Somewhere in her throat, a scream echoed as spiders swarmed and bound her body tightly in a cocoon.

Not a minute had passed before they were dragging her away.

"She will be well cared for!" said Ariadne, her chelicerae chittering as she spoke. She turned then to Bubo as if this too were his best chance to surrender.

"You *can't* be a spider," he said incredulously. "I spoke to you on the phone. You sounded like a leggy blonde."

Ariadne seemed to preen. "I know right? Sometimes we record phone calls for employee training purposes. When I listen to them, I'm like, Whoa, is that *my* voice? Crazy! I sound like Dolores from HR, not a three-thousand-year-old matriarch who challenged a goddess and forced her to bless me."

"You said that on the phone too. I thought you were joking. You seem to say that a lot."

"It is a legitimately impressive qualification."

"You mean that you challenged Athena at the loom? Because I'm a warrior. Women's work is of no interest to me, so—"

"You couldn't beat Hermes in a farting contest!" The hairs on her body bristled with rage. "You came to *my* house to steal the work of *my* daughters because without it you would have been killed today a thousand times over! On your idiotic 'man'-paign."

Bubo snarled. "Oh, I am so sick of this word! You wouldn't call Genghis Khan a man-paigner."

"I called him worse to his face! How dare you cast shade on what we do here. Your entire church couldn't match an hour of labor we do here in a lifetime. Yet all the slaughter you've accomplished today, know that my daughters and I could kill twice as many again before morning!"

"But . . . you are not going to, right?" inquired Victor.

"Can it, pizza breath," she scolded before turning back to Bubo. "You had your whole adventure planned so perfectly— only one tiny detail overlooked: how were you going to get out of the Euphorium with your prizes? In other words, *you had no plan at all.* This is a den of spiders! It is, by definition, a trap! Even if your maidens managed to overpower the Lavender Leek here, what then? What did you plan to do about us millions of deadly hunters watching your every step?"

"For all these," Bubo said smugly, "I have a rolled up newspaper."

"Onions aren't even a pizza topping, really," Victor interjected.

"On a good veggie slice, yes, people put onions!" snapped Ariadne.

"But for you, my dear Ariadne," said Bubo, "I have something special."

"How special can it be? Until five minutes ago you thought I was a leggy blonde."

Bubo tsk-tsked. "Smart remarks like that are why you've been a spinster for three millennia."

All eight of her eyes rolled. "I'm a spinster because *I challenged a goddess and forced her to bless me*! And you wonder why I say it so many fucking times!"

Bubo's spurs jangled as he walked toward her on the catwalk. "You have eight legs, Ariadne. I suggest you start using some of them to run."

Thousands of spiders chittered as they prepared to defend their queen.

"Stand down, my daughters. As the beefy bro in the movies says: I have got this."

Bubo tossed back his cape and removed something from his belt. "Behold the Axe of Spider Kill. Thus dubbed and anointed by the Arch-patriarch of the CKE." It sorta looked like a big scalloped Twinkie on a skewer.

"Oh, here comes the lictor!" cried Ariadne. "Think I haven't seen that before? Your angry-little-man toy has no power over me."

"Is that so? I propose an experiment."

With a backhand, Bubo brought the axehead down with all his weight on Ariadne's head. She didn't even flinch.

You know how when you have a spider in your kitchen and you clump up a paper towel and smash it for all you're worth? Got it! You must have because it disappeared. But then you check inside and there's no spider in there. So you look around the counter and—hey, there it is, making a dash for it! So you smash it again. You do this like ten times, each time exactly the same, and you are like, What the fuck, how have you not died already?

Nothing happened to Ariadne. The axe didn't bounce off, it didn't pass through, it didn't miss. It just didn't work. I don't even know what to tell you, it's just one of those things.

"Is it my turn yet?" Ariadne said, rubbing her palps together.

Bubo backed away in horror.

"Ah, good!" She spat at him.

Bubo screamed and dropped the axe. He turned and ran until he smashed his face into a wall, then he turned back with his hands raised and screamed some more.

A full cannonade of spinnerets stared him down. "No," he managed to cry before a diarrhea of webbing exploded at him from every direction, encasing him in a sticky mess, all except his head. He was pinned helplessly to the wall.

Ariadne skittered up to Bubo. "Say something disgusting to me," she said softly, caressing his cheek with one of her long forelegs. "I desire it very much."

Bubo stopped struggling. At her touch, he began to weep.

Sure, that's one way to do it, thought Victor. *Be a meter long horror, juicy-full of glue and poison, and of course they cry like babies. But where's the art, I ask.*

"What are you going to do to me?" sobbed Bubo.

"Me?" said Ariadne. "Nothing."

A large blue spider with a red splotch on its back descended slowly from the ceiling. It stopped in front of Bubo's face, glowing slightly with bioluminescence, as if radioactive.

"Lady Ariadne, do you mind if I take a brief statement from him before you continue?" Victor asked. "It's kind of my thing."

"Sorry, Violet Storm," said Ariadne. "The biomagnetic fields created by this many spiders will jam any digital equipment. Besides, your audience won't have the stomach for what we are about to witness."

Bubo's complexion paled a few shades.

"Are you sure?" said Victor. "Dodoville's into some pretty gruesome shit. I've tried to skeeve them out once or twice, but it didn't even faze them."

Ariadne turned sharply. "You are a guest in my house! Now have some manners and enjoy the entertainment!"

"A good host might bring out a chair," he said, as if to nobody. "Maybe a refreshment."

Ariadne ignored him.

233

"Please, my Queen," stammered Sir Bubo. "We at the CKE always meant to pay you. Whatever price you name, you'll get it. Accept a down payment. Please."

"This is all the payment we require. For the silks you already stole!"

"How did they get those exactly," asked Victor, "if security here is as tight as you say?"

"You are going to feel a pinch," Ariadne informed Bubo.

The glowy blue spider stabbed a foreleg into Bubo's right cheek. The flesh convulsed in pain. Gradually, the twitching subsided as that half of his face entered paralysis. The jaw locked, fastening that corner of his mouth open at a few centimeters. On the other side of his face, the eye opened in terror as Bubo whimpered for mercy.

Ariadne turned to Victor.

"The Elizabethans used to say, if you see the spider in your cup before you swallow it, you shall surely die. It sounds like superstition but . . . Do you want to know why they believed that?"

"Pleathe," blubbered Bubo, his tongue thick from the neurotoxin. "The Church will be your thlaveth. We'll worthip you as the one true god. Harthur? Who'th that guy? He thoundth made up!"

The blue-glowing spider stabbed a foreleg into the other cheek, injecting another dose of poison. Once again, half of Bubo's face twitched violently and then came to complete rest, like a bug zapped by roach spray.

The only animate part left of Bubo was the eyeballs, which watched the spider's egg-shaped body intently.

Using its eight legs like cranes, it lowered its body into Bubo's frozen jaw. The Onion thought he could hear the metallic hairs of the legs scraping against Bubo's teeth. The hairy body rose several times in and out of Bubo's mouth as if it was scratching itself on the tongue.

"What's it doing?" asked Victor.

"I'm not giving you the Animal Planet narration!"

"Seriously, though."

"Stimulating the salivary glands."

"Ew. Why?"

"You have eyes enough to watch!"

The two rearmost legs stabbed under the jaw. The throat began to contract repeatedly. Slowly, one joint a time, the legs followed the body into the maw. For a long moment, nothing happened. Then the eyelids fluttered open and Bubo's breath caught. The twitch in the neck continued. Victor could see the bulge of the spider in the throat as Bubo choked. Then the passageway cleared and the knight again drew breath.

"How do you train your soldier to do that?" Victor asked.

"What do you mean?"

"What incentive did you give that spider to sacrifice herself like that? I'm not judging, just curious."

"Nothing, actually," said Ariadne. "That's just how spiders are. They see a human orifice—a mouth, a nostril, a butthole— their instinct is to crawl right in and die there."

"No."

"Any hole at all. Even an open wound! Can't hardly resist. Usually, though, we wait till you're asleep."

"Funny," Victor said, "but not that funny."

"I mean, even I feel the lure," she said, a drop of venom falling from her palps. "Think of the cost to me. For millennia, I have been pursuing a plan for global power. All that time and energy, accumulating knowledge and influence, waiting for the right opportunities. But then I take one look at you . . ."

"Stop!"

"Listen. I'm a big girl," she said teasingly, "but I can fit myself in some tight spaces. Maybe after this, we can get a drink or two, and later if we're having a good time—"

"You're trying to make me uncomfortable."

Ariadne made a non-committal noise, brushing her cephalothorax "accidentally" against him. "Watch now, darling. It's starting."

Suddenly, Bubo retched. Up came a mess of grape cola and corn chips.

"Gross," said Victor, indulgently.

Vomiting was a typical part of the lacrimation ritual. It had never bothered him, but he wanted to seem polite.

A dribble of blood appeared on Bubo's lip and poured out in a thin cascade. It blackened as it flowed.

"Do you like tripe?" the spider asked inquisitively.

The chunks came in spurts, covered in dark blood.

"That's . . . not partially digested food."

236

Ariadne's drool hit the catwalk with a hiss. "No. Do you like tripe?" she repeated.

"No, and I don't like sweetbreads either!"

Ariadne's surprisingly musical laugh rang out.

"Wrigglety, jiggelty, tickledy spider!" she sang.

"You have a beautiful voice."

"Of course I do. You can't weave for three thousand years without a way to make the time pass. 'Who can say why-der he swallowed the spider? He's not even a fy-der!'"

Something dark and spongy fell out of the mouth and hit the catwalk with a wet plop.

"There's your sweetbread, my treat!"

Victor watched in fascination. "What does this? What did you inject him with?"

"Inject?"

"Chemical. Enzyme, neurotransmitter. To cause this reaction."

Ariadne shook her head. "No chemicals. Just plain old howling fantods."

"Who?"

"Skeevies. Creepies. Fear, dread, gross-out yuck. It's a reflex."

"How can it be a reflex? Surely he's dead by now?"

"Don't be dull. Once the body crosses a threshold of agony it becomes impossible for it to die for a while. I promise you he feels all of this."

"I'm pretty sure that's heart."

"Could be. Anyways, bones last."

"What do you mean, 'Bones last'?" cried Victor. "There'd be nothing to force them out if only bones were left!"

"'Bones last' is what I mean 'bones last!' Anyhow, let's away. Unless you want to watch a man spit up his own skull?"

She was asking. It was an honest question.

"Not if I can't have video footage, no."

Ariadne laughed again. "Biomagnetic interference! You are such a dumbass."

"Oh come on! I suffered a severe science-related trauma as a child!"

"I have to trick you somehow. Here you are in my lair, a highly trained warrior in invincible and *incredibly* skintight body armor. You are welcome by the way."

"That reminds me, I'd really like to know—"

"And also, thank *you*," said Ariadne, leering out of at least six of her eight eyes.

"—how the Pestilence got enough silk for four horses. I had to sell a fleet of traffic helicopters to pay for mine."

"Leave a girl her secrets, won't you?" she giggled, wiggling her opisthosoma at the pedicel.

"I really could have used video of a confession from Bubo. To show the wicked of Dodoville what happens when I'm outnumbered eight to one."

"Wasn't your very public triumph at the joust enough?"

"For today, yes. But sometimes a crime fighter has a slow streak.

Plus it's the least you could have done after I cleaned out your . . . infestation."

"I owe you no debt, vigilante! The Violet Storm exists at *my* pleasure."

"I could say Ariadne the Weaver now exists at mine! It's not as you say. You would not have had as easy a time with those shieldmaidens as you had with Bubo Skymole."

"So you say. Yet I did rescue you, vigilante. So I hope you don't intend to leave tonight without giving me a thank you kiss."

Victor eyed the spider, trying to gauge if she was serious.

"I'm not really inclined to um . . ."

Ariadne stiffened. "Watch how you finish that sentence if you like your innards on the inside."

"Compromise my identity."

"Take that mask off, Victor Cumin," she said, stroking his hip with her tarsus. "You have no secrets from me."

"But cameras do work in here. I don't want to be blackmailed tomorrow."

She seemed to smile at him. "After all the dangers you faced today, you fear the desire of a . . . needful woman?"

"This is a spider's den," said Victor. "As you said before, it is by definition a trap."

Ariadne giggled. "Which is only fun if you let yourself get caught in it. Listen, there's nothing I can do to you that I need your permission for. But I'm asking your consent. Just a regular girl who wants a taste of your affection. Don't I deserve it? After all, I fought for you, I protected you, and for heaven's sake, I *dressed* you! Besides. Aren't I the most beautiful of my kind?"

In truth, Victor supposed he had never seen eyes so large, so purple, so . . . quantinous on a woman before.

"You want to know how the Pestilence got those silks?" asked Ariadne teasingly. "Well, have you thought about how *hard* it is to get you here? We weave you a miracle material, and you send that stuffy old skiapod to pick it up. We don't even get to take your measurements. My daughters and I offer free tailoring services!"

"I hope you're not suggesting . . . Many people died today!"

"The atrocities which these knights committed, they had been planning for nearly a century: it was only ever a matter of time. But today, you not only defeated them, you humiliated them and destroyed any pretense they had to honorable intent."

Victor thought about this. It made a modicum of sense, but . . .

"And you looked really cool doing it," Ariadne continued. "Flying through the sky. Riding your motorbike. Rocking that ssssexy jumpsuit."

"How pathetic you sound!" Victor spat. "All that carnage today just so you could . . . could . . ."

Ariadne sighed. "See, *this* is why you should have let us measure you. The skiapod sewed your underpants too tight: that's why you can't enjoy a perfectly good ego-stroking moment. No, it wasn't just to flirt with you. As the matriarch of the arachnids, I don't have the luxury of being quite *that* selfish. But yes, today was just for you. Your various escapades around town—you have just produced, starred in, and are about to distribute internationally the most compelling advertisement for the featherweight, invincible armor my daughters and I make here. And when resources begin flowing in from around the world, the humans who rule Dodoville shall know they do so at *my pleasure.*"

The glistening spider took four steps forward toward the Purple Onion, (which was basically one step but with a lot more bristling of spines) and whispered.

"And today, my pleasure will be a kiss from the handsome man who defended me from the naughty-waughty knight who twied to steal my pwetty cwothes!"

She swayed and hummed seductively. The melody seemed just beyond the threshold of recognition as if he could almost but not quite put words to it.

Wrigglety, jiggelty, tickledy.

One by one, Bubo's ribs were rising out of his mouth in fluid motion. Kind of hypnotic to watch in its way.

Down on the factory floor, someone was still axing away at the loom.

EPISODE SEVEN:

THE HARROWING CRY AT HOME

IN THE OBSERVATORY atop Davy Castle's west tower, Victor Cumin sat at his desk, reading the morning papers. His literal-goddamn-everything hurt. Even for the Violet Storm, the previous day had been particularly fight-intensive. He'd nearly been struck by a missile, too.

Though no sore or bruise compared to the blistering itchy skin issue he had developed overnight. The salves and unguents from the medicine chest didn't seem to help.

"Looks like you were the 'Victor' again last night, sir!"

Victor resisted the impulse to cover up. This was his house, and he'd scratch himself whenever or wherever he saw fit. He just wished Mori would announce himself before he entered a room. Or wear a bell.

Victor threw the copy of the *Spyhole* on the desk casually as if his fingernails had not just been administering some brutal self-satisfaction to his inner thigh. He tapped a finger on one of the headlines.

"Can you believe some people think we staged all the battles yesterday as a popular entertainment?"

"I keep forgetting your species considers it fun to show each other the insides of your skulls." The butler's smile was full of inexplicable warmth. "But everyone says it was a pretty good show, Master Victor."

Mori set a small jar of ointment on the desk in front of him. Probably a concoction of jungle horrors, but his track record with exotic medical treatments suggested it would neutralize whatever was irritating his skin.

Victor opened the editorial section to the "Ask a Dodo Anything" feature.

"It seems some voices around town are salty about how the manor houses up in Prismton got their own private viewing."

"Now, Master Victor. The very same people would be complaining if you'd driven the Bratmobile into low-income housing."

Victor took a sniff of what was inside the jar. Like death itself had died of ass rot. In a hot damp place.

"Bratmobile? Is that really what they're calling it."

"It is a rather wienery-looking vehicle, sir."

Victor shrugged. No man with the freedom to do so would own fewer than one wiener-shaped automobile, he thought.

"Still," he said, "That crash wouldn't have happened if civilians didn't own anti-horse ballistas."

"Some people would say the real injustice is that ordinary hard-working Dodovilleans didn't get a chance to field test *their* ballistas. They pay taxes too, you know."

Whatever was in this stench pot felt pretty good on his skin, actually.

"No one living in modern society needs a computer-targeted spear chucker!"

"The Cumin estate has two, for the record," said Mori.

"Why? The only horses around here are mother's Lusitanos. Throw them out." He slathered the ointment everywhere it itched, i.e. everywhere. "The ballistas, not the horses, of course."

"Digital targeting is tricky, Master Victor. Sometimes it saves time to study how others have solved the problem instead of reinventing the wheel."

"Throw them out or you're fired. Also, I've already forgotten about this."

"Very good, sir."

"By the way, Mori: that weird lasso stick you built me? It really came through."

"Of course it did, sir. My people designed it for master warriors at the dawn of history."

"If skiapods are so averse to self-defense, how'd they become such geniuses at weaponry?"

Mori shrugged. "You might as well ask an Olympic champion swimmer how they got so good at walking. Some things are just easy."

Like wanting to murder skiapods, Victor thought.

"So, I have another question."

"Shoot, sir."

"How come you never told me you acquired my body armor form an enormous talking spider?"

Mori smiled sadly with all the wisdom of however the hell many years old Mori was. "To me, Lady Ariadne is just a person, sir. You forget, over my long life, I've dwelt in shadows with all sorts of sapient beings whom the human world thinks of as monsters. But we've lived on earth longer than you have—and if I can be frank, some of us will be here after you're gone. And that has earned us, if nothing else, the right to consider ourselves people, with or without the human world's permission."

"I see your point." Victor was pensive. "I also saw a man vomit up his own skull."

Mori nodded. "I recommend remaining on Lady Ariadne's good side."

"I don't even know how to describe it. The eyes remained in their sockets, but the sockets came out his mouth."

"Spiders' ways are not our ways."

"I have another question. If you knew Ariadne could crush any band of marauding thieves, why did you send me there?"

"I wanted you to see, sir. As the defender of Dodoville, I wanted you to know where your power comes from. I wanted you to treat that with the proper awe and respect. Sir, you have taken an awesome responsibility upon yourself, so remember you are this city's servant, not its master. Remember it for your own sake, as much as others'."

"Those are wise words, Mori," said Victor, not understanding at all.

"Also, I figured you'd have a lot of fun." Mori smiled.

"Spiders *are* awesome," said Victor. "I've always known that, but I had no idea."

He watched Mori pretend to dust the console to the observatory's mammoth sound telescope. Really, he was inputting instructions for Ladybird to gather intel for the Violet Storm's next mission.

Which reminded him.

"I don't understand it, Mori. Since my mother's death, I've been developing the perfect vigilante persona, the perfect symbol of righteous vengeance. The Violet Storm. Listen how the words roll off the tongue. You even hear a pleasant crash of thunder in the silence that follows."

"That's the coffeemaker."

"And the color! It's the same otherworldly shade as Mt. Myrtle's fulminations. Not *onion*. More like an ube, if anything."

"You really don't want to be called The Purple Yam. May I make a recommendation, Master Victor? When people love you, accept the love they give. Do not try to force it into a shape it is not. If they see a lion, be a lion. If they see a storm, be a storm."

"But they see a vegetable, Mori!"

247

"Remember, sir, that the onion is an emblem of all of us. Every person, be they human, skiapod, sapient spider, or giant magma slug that awakens once every thousand years—"

"Wait, what?"

"—each has one thing in common. They all cry."

Oh, that *was* the coffeemaker.

"Not me, Mori. I don't cry. Not since the day my mother succumbed to that atomic virus."

"Even you, sir. The path you have chosen is long and dark. I cannot tell you where it will lead, only that you will find tears at the end of it."

"Is that some weird skiapod power? Knowing the future."

"Just the power of growing old. I have seen a lot of suffering in my time. Enough to know I shall see a lot more."

Victor nodded. If he lived long enough, one day he too could look forward to casting gloomy clouds over everybody's life.

"What have you got in your hand?" he asked.

Mori brought forth the envelope he'd been hiding behind his back. "It is a summons, sir."

"Summons? Didn't we already pay off the police this quarter?"

"From the solarium, sir."

Davy Castle's east tower. Victor swallowed down a groan as he opened the letter. "Written in his own blood again, I see."

"Your father is nothing if not practical."

The words "SEE ME" had been smeared on the page with a thumb.

"Todd always confounded the pragmatic with the melodramatic."

"In either case, sir, I wouldn't leave him waiting too long."

•

Victor took the east elevator up to the solarium. He managed to control his breathing but barely felt the car start or stop on its slow rise up the tower.

The button light went dark, signaling his arrival. The doors opened under a cavernous enclosure.

The walls were tetrahedral glass topped with a pyramid, like the apex of an obelisk.

In the early '90s, when prosperity had paid a visit to Dodoville, when science stood at the helm of state and art flowered in the loam of research and learning, this chamber had been the ecstatic center of the city. During the day, the sun poured through the glass panels onto a garden of prismatic flowers that exploded into color to mark the hours. At night, the solarium hosted grand balls with live orchestras, while vast and vibrant mountain starscapes hung above like a chandelier. And in the center of the room, atop its earthen pedestal, a live oak, strong and verdant, had stood as if the anchor between earth and sky.

The tree was dead now, a dark splintering husk that spread its branches like vulture's wings. Black curtains shrouded the rise of the pyramid as if a dragon had devoured the light of heaven to the last spark. You could still see the mountains in the distance, but the view outside came no longer through the glass but from an array of flatscreen monitors. They displayed the countryside not in its current mid-morning splendor but at murky dusk with Mt. Myrtle fulminating irritably in the distance. Carotene tendrils which lashed out into the night offered the only splashes of color over the black-and-white terrain.

The scenery harbingered the end, an apocalypse which for Todd Cumin already lay in the past.

Victor's shoes echoed across marble tiles towards where his father sat in his wheelchair. Not even before the sky joust did his muscles clench with trepidation as they did now. He felt as if he were entering not the presence of the man who sired him but his temple, built in memory of a legendary era that had never quite existed.

His father had seldom left here since the incident, now ten years in the past.

Victor followed a path that ventured through the garden of glass flowers and stopped before the henge of control panels and monitors that kept his father's body alive. The largest machine was performing its bizarre dialysis on him, drawing purplish-black fluid from his veins into transfusion tubes. After passing through a centrifuge, the toxin produced in Todd's marrow was expelled as a fine dark powder. It fell, grain-by-grain, into a gold container, the miracle substance his body produced at an astounding rate.

The dying emperor in perverse symbiosis with his dying empire.

Todd Cumin had today's *Spyhole* across his lap. The ceases were not sharp. It had been pored over with attention and rage.

The sick man coughed wetly into a handkerchief, pulling away a splotch of dark sputum. Victor stood and waited, his aid or greeting neither expected nor desired. Todd had surely recognized his step, distinct from either the nurse's tread or Mori' fleshy leaps. But Victor couldn't shake the feeling this whole tower was a crippled golem alive with his father's consciousness, the frail body before him merely the tattered written word that gave it animation.

For a long moment, he listened to the older Cumin's machine-aided breath. It seemed to emerge out of another dimension, another reality.

See me, the summons had read. As if the demand had been to witness the twisted shell he'd become. See the ghost haunting the east tower (by whatever rationale still called a solarium), the ghost who also haunted the *Spyhole*, whose pages Todd now went out into the world as a part of, just as the *Spyhole* had long been part of Todd.

"Citroën von Chesterdrawer is a genius," croaked the shattered voice. "Make sure nobody ever finds out, or they'll install him as chief of one of the capital city rags before we can make a counteroffer."

The feature photo on the front page showed Victor's alter ego unhorsing Sir Heckley midair. The knight's jawline remained in focus as the blow carried him backward, open-armed over the rear of his mount. A nice capture in rich violet and gold.

"With stories like this one," Victor said, "even the U Dodo daily could sell out its morning edition."

"Cumin Media is your birthright," crackled Todd's voice. "Its fate will be your legacy. Not this circus show you put on last night."

Victor raised his eyebrows. "You think that was me?"

"Who else would be jumping a motorcycle in my late wife's slippers?"

That Todd knew the identity of the Violet Storm should have come as no surprise. Nonetheless, Victor felt suddenly off-balance.

"Rochelle's fashion choices still have a lot of fans," he observed. "It could be anyone."

"Those were her personal bedroom attire."

Victor watched years-old footage of the volcano fling a ball of molten rock into the sky. "What can I say. Fans."

Todd's pounded the armrest of his chair. "You may not disgrace the Horsefolk! They are Dodoville's history—its noble, most ancient tradition. When visitors come here, they want to hear how before the age of industry, people here drank the blood of mares and defied the Catholic priests. How Dodovilleans are descended from the chivalrous knights of Europe and heirs to the Round Table."

"In other words," said Victor, "they want to laugh at the delusions of uneducated locals."

"Let them."

"Those Horsefolk were barbarians in every sense. Lawless, illiterate brutes. The ones that cling to that legacy today are no better. Why are we honoring them? All it gets us is a fiasco like yesterday's."

Todd's corrupted blood had stained his lips and jaw so black, he had given up trying to remove it.

"And what a profitable fiasco if you hadn't interfered! Selling these fables to foreigners is what wealth this city has. It gives strength to the Consortium, which maintains order. Which prevents the city from disintegrating into the chaos of yet another gang war. Or have you forgotten how our family fared in the last one?"

Victor reflected first on the laboratory-designed disease that had killed Rochelle, then on the strange affliction that would one day claim Todd. Few people on earth could afford to die such exotic deaths as his parents—the price tag of their assassinations was simply too high! This exclusivity formed a bond between Todd and his late wife even now.

"Of course I remember," said Victor.

"The Consortium is the peace your mother and I worked for. That your mother died for. If you challenge its authority in this city, either in the newspaper or . . . in your leotards, not only will you be defeated, but you will destroy everything she and I have worked for."

Victor stepped in front of his father, blocking his view of Mt.

Myrtle fulminating on the screen. The old man's eyes tried to find a path to the images behind him.

"Look at me, Todd. It was the Consortium who did this to you. Who sabotaged your printing press, who poisoned your marrow so you'd cough up and bleed your own company ink."

The old man shook his head, casting his glance down and away.

"That's a convenient thing to believe, son. It also happens not to be true."

"Face the facts. It couldn't have been anyone else. You choose to believe what you want to believe!"

The old man's eyes now focused on nothing, as if having willed themselves to blindness.

"Me, is it? I'm the one who believes in fairy tales, am I? Yet you are about to tell me how your mother would have supported this insane vigilantism of yours. The way you disgrace all of us, the prestige of our entire industry!"

Victor believed Todd had always been trying to drive a wedge between his wife and son while she was alive—out of fear the two would turn against him together. It was an exquisite agony that his father still attempted to do this now, twenty years after her death.

"Unlike you," Victor said, "Rochelle always adapted to the times. She seized new opportunities, and she cut away the dead weight of the past. That's what I'm doing."

"You are tearing this city apart. Tearing Cumin Media apart!"

Inky blood dribbled from his lip as he cried out.

Victor leaned on the arms of his father's wheelchair, trying to meet his evading eyes. "The Consortium sells relics from an age we have already turned our backs on. It is *literally* the past. This city needs a path with a future!"

"There is no future anymore," Todd grumbled.

"No," Victor said sadly. "Not for you, there isn't."

"Not for anyone." Todd's voice was more forceful now. "Not in Dodoville. History has passed us over. That is what you refuse to accept!"

The classic Dodoville defeatism, unshakable here since the fourteenth century.

"That's a lie. If you opened those windows, if you looked at today's living city instead of fixating on this memory of the past, you'd see it. Dodoville is ready to lead the world into the future instead of following so many centuries behind. But it needs our help first to set it free. It needs the Violet Storm."

Todd wriggled his fragile shoulders in mockery. He tried to laugh, but the effort exhausted him. Raising only a bubble of blood, his humor turned to rage.

"Dodoville doesn't change," he said. "The volcano stays irritable and angry, and we remain at the precipice of annihilation. It makes us impulsive, full of secret fears and consumed by ancient anger. Rochelle couldn't see this because she was a foreigner. And you. You can't see it because you're an idiot."

Victor leaned close enough to whisper in his father's ear. The skin was paper-thin and riddled with black veins.

"The difference between you and me is, I'm out there. And you're in here watching old video on loop."

Todd's body shuddered as he clenched a hand into a fist. "I have put my blood in the *Spyhole*! My blood will not betray me!"

"You don't have blood anymore. You're just a dirty old inkpot."

"And you! What are you?" For the first time, Todd looked at him fully. "The angels who guard the tombs of our ancestors weep . . . for shame!"

The Violet Storm priding himself in his unrelenting calm. If only Victor could hold on to that sangfroid now.

"Enjoy the rest of your life," he said softly. "Such that is it."

Victor turned to walk out. Once again his footsteps echoed on the marble tile.

"Hey, Acting President of Cumin Media. Do you know why every reporter at every news outlet in the city calls you the Purple Onion? Because if they don't, they know they'll never work here again!"

Victor stopped.

"That's right. It's me, you smug son of a bitch. Me!"

So there it is, thought Victor. *The old ogre is still calling the shots.*

"Oh, you know it, baby!" cried Todd in his chair, his broken voice carrying over a microphone he had activated on his chair. "This is still *my* town."

Victor entered the waiting elevator and pressed the button to close the doors.

"Or do you think no one can stop you?" Todd's voice

persisted. "I'll stop you. You're just an onion! Hear me? A purple. Fucking. Onion!"

In a fit of anger, Victor balled a fist and punched out the ceiling light. In the darkness of the car, there was no possibility for mistake. Twin pinpricks of gold light had appeared in his pupils.

"You are goddamn right," he said.

THANK YOU FOR READING!

I sincerely appreciate you taking the time to join me on this insane adventure into the crime world of Dodoville. It was a true joy to write, and I hope you enjoyed it as well.

Let me take this chance to remind you that independent authors like myself rely greatly on reviews from readers, so please consider leaving a sentence or two about your experience with this book wherever you purchase books online. It really does means a lot!

I'd love to hear from you! Feel free to contact me at silverstrigil.net where you can share your comments or questions. You can also sign up for my reading group for bonus material, giveaways, artwork, and information about future books.

ABOUT THE AUTHOR

I am a Nashville based writer, and a proud native of the Bronx, New York. I hold a degree in something ridiculous from a fancy institution of higher education. (Hint: it's classical studies at Penn.) By day I perform manual labor so that by night I have enough brain power left to deliver the hard-hitting truths about the struggles of imaginary monsters. I study foreign languages for fun. All my pets are house plants.

ABOUT THE AUTHOR

www.ingramcontent.com/pod-product-compliance
Lightning Source LLC
Chambersburg PA
CBHW021002120726
47905CB00009B/2814